A Lime Jewel

A LIME JEWEL

AN ANTHOLOGY OF POETRY
AND SHORT STORIES
IN AID OF HAITI

FOREWORD BY NII AYIKWEI PARKES

EDITED BY
YETUNDE RUBAN

BlackLondoner Appeal

Assistant Editors: Caroline Obonyo & Jacqueline Auma

First published in Great Britain in 2010
By BlackLondoner Appeal
9 Grenaby Road
CR0 2EJ

©Contributors 2010
Yetunde Ruban

All rights reserved
No part of this publication may be reproduced or transmitted in any form without permission

ISBN 978-0-9566748-0-7

Cover image: 'Reflections of Hope' by ©Kemi Aderibigbe

Book jacket design by Danielle Humphrey www.leapers.co.uk

ACKNOWLEDGEMENTS

Simon Murray: "Reparation Song– poetry in book, Abeng Soundings: Abolitionist Landmarks of Our Freedom-march – S2007B, 2008; AAAAAAAAAAAAAAAAARGHHHH! – poetry in anthology, FWords: Creative Freedom – Peepal Tree Press, 2007

CONTENTS

Foreword: Nii Ayikwei Parkes   13

Preface: Yetunde Ruban   15

PART 1

Haitian Revolution   18
Christine-Jean Blain

Haiti   19
Stacey Lois Howard

They Came From Beyond the Waves   21
Rene Thomas

Chanson de la liberation- a blues for Haiti   23
Kamara Muntu

Scorpion sting in my rhythm   24
Mbizo Charisha

Blackology II   25
Lloyd Akinsanya

Aaaaaaaaaaaaaaaaarghhhh!   27
Simon Murray

Reparation Song   31
Simon Murray

The Brain Burning   33
Deka Ibrahim

Haiti   34
Bob McNeil

Long Line of Runners (Lifetime 1) **Christine-Jean Blain**	36
Come See **Sophia Wilson**	38
Still **Tolu Ogunlesi**	39
Haiti Morning Coffee **Suzanne V Creavalle**	41

PART 2

Breaking News **Stephanie L. Kemp**	44
I Saw the Rubble **Jeffrey Jaiyeola**	45
Where All Mankind Treads **Andy Nguyen**	46
After (the) shock **Yolanda M Dean**	47
For The Mother and Child **Ann Margaret Lim**	48
The Aftermath **Opal Minott**	49
A Real True Nightmare **Tanya Leon**	50
Heartless Earth **Uche Francis Uwadinachi**	52
Haiku Poem – Haiti **Lucreta La Pierre**	54

The Nameless **Nadine Pinede**	55
Celeste **Tade Thompson**	57
Wake Up Haiti!! **Marcia Kay Ellis**	61
Haiti Earthquake Aftermath, Journal Entries **Kathuska Jose**	63
Kijan m santim **Erline Vendredi**	64
Hope For Haiti Requiem For Haiti **Fitzroy Cole**	68 69
Nothing Makes Sense Anymore **Geoffrey Philp**	70
Why Me? **Tony Walsh**	71
The Unnatural Order Of Things **Stephanie Kemp**	72
Earth Trembling **Alexander Thanni**	73
Haiti **Akilah Moseley**	75
Haiti Lost **Acquaye McCalman**	76
Soon **Uche Francis Uwadinachi**	77

PART 3

A Lime Jewel **Nadifa Mohamed**	80
11 Days After the Quake **Maroula Blades**	82
Rising of the Morning Sun **Stacey Lois Howard**	85
Life **Nick Falconer**	87
A Prayer for Haiti **Esther Ackah**	88
Singing our Own Song **Kwame M A McPherson**	89
My Haiti **Nicole Weaver**	91
Catching the tap-tap to Cayes-de-Jacmel **Lane Ashfeldt**	92
Something of an Apology **RaShell R. Smith-Spears**	98
Rise Up Haiti **Phil Gregory**	99
Survivor **Olufemi Amao**	101
Ode to Haiti **Georgina Jackson-Callen**	102
The Ripened Faith **Nash Colundalur**	104

Haiti Strong **Margaret Danquah**	105
Sankofa **Lloyd Akinsanya**	106
Wake Up To Haiti **Jai Ellis-Crook**	109
Haiti My Generation **Mbizo Chirasha**	110
Does Life Have a Purpose **David Larbi**	112
He **Abigail Perry Duah**	113
I Know That it May Hurt **LaTrell Johnson**	114
True Spirit **Kathy Cakebread**	116
Serpent and the Rainbow **Christine-Jean Blain**	117
What Matters Most **Stacey Lois Howard**	121
Sympathy **Paul Laurence Dunbar**	123
Notes	124
Contributors	125

FOREWORD

A Lime Jewel: Word for Haiti

Tragedy has no restraint, no sense of fairness, no inkling of justice; it comes and goes and asks no questions. In its wake, grief makes the strongest of us shiver as we come to terms with what is lost, what is broken – broken homes, broken bones, broken tongues. For who knows what to say when a new year, a time of beginnings, brings an earthquake such as the one that has scarred the beautiful half of Hispaniola that is Haiti. Yet it is with our broken tongues that we must ask the questions that tragedy did not, that we must speak order back into our world. This collection of musings, poems, stories, dialogue, monologue and song, *A Lime Jewel*, seeks to do precisely that.

The work contained here represents the entire gamut of human reaction to tragedy; half-formed to fully-formed, brash to quiet, resigned to frustrated. But it also contains work given simply as gifts – not commentary on the fact, the brutal reality of Haiti's wounded, dead and orphaned – work given as a contribution to the long-term work of rebuilding Haiti in image and in fact. *A Lime Jewel* is a love song of prickles and polish, that bristles with the urgency of a towncrier, swells with the patience of a mother and hums with the wisdom of a village elder: while 15-year-old Acquaye McCalman announces in the poem, 'Haiti Lost,' "I see a flow of tragedy", and Stephanie L. Kemp in 'Breaking News' speaks of "Corrugated roofs/ Rippling like waves at high tide"; there are those, like Nadine Pinede who are already looking beyond the news, the made-for-primetime footage that shapes our imagination of tragedy – her poem, 'The Nameless,' mindful of our short memories, cautions us "For every face the cameras do not capture/ there is a name and memories/ of murmured songs half-remembered.../ Remember this, when the show is over/ and you/ turn away."

This collection, to my mind, is buttressed by important reminders that Haiti did not come into existence the moment the world became aware of its plight. As Nadifa Mohamed indicates in the title poem,

'A Lime Jewel,' there is a rich history: "asleep beneath the tarmac/ black Jacobins." Yes, the earthquake came and took lives and buildings, it swallowed dreams and families, but it can not take away Haiti's proud past. Haiti was a pioneer in the New World, winning its independence from France in 1804 to become – alongside Ethiopia – a black African state not occupied, colonised or listed (falsely or actually) as a protectorate. The rebellions that led to Haiti's independence, like the January 2010 earthquake, cost lives in the hundreds of thousands, but the agreements that followed after Toussaint L'Ouverture had been betrayed and imprisoned in France (imposed by massive military threats by the French) also cost Haiti its financial autonomy, leaving it at the mercy of mercenary European banks. It is not right for Haiti to have to beg for aid; let us not forget that. *A Lime Jewel* is a much more dignified way to contribute to the rehabilitation of Haiti than some meaningless, guilt-erasing handouts, something that will live longer than the interest of the media, the studied pity of strangers.

As Sophia Wilson declares in 'Come See' "Though now a part of our great history/ this earthquake does not define Haiti/ Hey cousin come see"

Nii Ayikwei Parkes

PREFACE

"I saw the dying boys in the arms of dead fathers": Jeffrey Jaiyeola's lament in his poem *I saw the Rubble,* resonates with everyone who witnessed the images of despair and destruction caused by the Haiti earthquake of 12 January 2010. No one who saw those images could remain unmoved by the plight of the Haitian people. Many of us reached into our pockets and donated what we could but as the stories of the disaster unfolded, so did the gnawing question: Why? Political analysts, religious zealots and all manner of self-styled pundits all too eagerly offered their analysis, and as Jeffrey noted, their solutions would all too often "blame the woes of Haiti on Toussaint/Praise the foes of Haiti and call them saints". All of us involved in the project acknowledge that Haiti is more than the sum total of its disasters. Haiti was the birth place of Black emancipation; Haiti gave us our right to self-determination.

Hence this project grew out of a desire to stand in solidarity with the Haitian people long after the cameras were gone, a desire to acknowledge the true place of Haiti and its people in the emancipation of all black people and the fight for justice and freedom for all. As such, *A Lime Jewel* has been an intensely personal journey for all of us who have been involved in this project. For me it has been a labour of love, a journey of discovery.

As Editor, I have to thank all those who answered our call for submissions and sent in their contributions. We received over 300 submissions from all over the world, including poetry, prose, short stories, free verse, photographs, paintings, illustrations and songs. It was difficult to whittle these down to the final 60 pieces which make up the anthology. We felt that every submission deserved to be part of the anthology but alas, we were constrained by costs. Thus each piece was carefully considered, until we arrived at a combination we felt reflected what we want this anthology to represent.

Special thanks go to my accomplices, Caroline Obonyo and Jacquie Auma, who were members of the editorial team and helped with the selection process – without them this anthology would not have been possible. We are also indebted to Nii Ayikwei Parkes who kindly agreed to write the foreword to this anthology.

The anthology is divided into three parts, each part serving as a loose grouping that we hope will help guide you through the collection. The first part is a celebration of Haitian history, Haiti, the Land where negritude first stood on its feet[*], the birthplace of proud black men who demanded liberty or death. The defiance in Murray's poems encapsulates the Haitian spirit whilst Christine-Jean Blain's loving opening reminds us of women's contribution in the Haitian struggle for independence and self determination.

The works contained in the second section describe the depth of feeling about the earthquake disaster of 12 January 2010. This is a moving aspect of current Haitian history and it was one of the more challenging parts to put together, in that there was so much outpouring of feelings and emotions which will remain with us for a long time. Part three looks to a future informed by the indomitable spirit of the Haitian people and underscored by the contributions of many of our young writers, LaTrell Johnson, Abigail Perry Duah, and others. We hope you enjoy this anthology and thank you all for your support.

Arise Haiti, look to your history and take your true place in the world. Viva Haiti!

Yetunde Ruban
London 2010
www.blacklondonerappeal.com

---

[*] *Courtesy,* **Aimé Fernand David Césaire** *(26 June 1913 – 17 April 2008)*

PART 1

There cannot exist slaves on this territory, servitude is therein forever abolished. All men are born, live and die free and French

Art 3, Haitian Constitution 1801

HAITIAN REVOLUTION

My Great-Great Grandmother told me
The Haitian revolution began when
The women told the men

*"If the plantation don't burn tonight
then we conceive no more children.
one way or another the suffering
will come to an end,
and if you won't light a match
then I'll have to cross my legs.*

*'Cause for too long you've been kissed by the lips of heaven,
for us to still be living in this hell.
And baby, understand well,
it will kill me to deny my man
but I rather sew shut the gates of this blessing before I birth
another field hand…
chambermaid…
or house slave."*

Christine-Jean Blain

HAITI

Emblazoned within
The black sands
Of molding hands
Black Powder
Decorating the Earth
To capture
Those departed
Left
Deserted
To fly back to the light
Wind blows
Rustling the souls
Of children
Beneath unseen crowns
Thrones
Of the dust that sustains them
Rearranges them
I was there
Hundreds of years ago
Arms outstretched
Laughing the laughter of a million sunrises
Barefoot and free
Feeling the dryness of the earth
On my fingertips
Midnight glow
Designing black hips
The fruit of the roots
Dripping juice on my lips
Before stolen
To cultivate the stolen land
Cultivating it
With the confusion of sorrow
Memories faded
Yet still outlined in the brightness
Of the soul of the ocean

Reflecting cast-away stones
And unclaimed bones
Conducting the sun
To cast the true light
Upon forgotten
Haiti

Stacey Lois Howard

THEY CAME FROM BEYOND THE WAVES

When they came in their ships
We met on the beach,
They were sick of the sea,
But too weary to leave,
And they brought me their gifts
Of fire and drink,
But their mercy meant more,
I was scared of their skin.

> They took too many liberties,
> Nothing's been the same since that day on the beach.
> And I thought they were gods
> Of the land that I owned,
> When they made me a prince,
> When they crowned me with thorns.

Well, their language is strange,
And my alphabet's good,
But they want it replaced,
So I'll be understood,
And they bit on the gold
I brought them for sale,
And they danced with my wives,
And they tore off their veils.

> They took too many liberties,
> Nothing's been the same since that day on the beach.
> And I thought they were gods
> Of the land that I owned,
> When they made me a prince,
> When they crowned me with thorns.

When the moon's in the sky,
They invited me to tea,
With my gold and my wives,
To the ships on the beach,
So I poisoned the gold
With a venom so fierce,
And the veils of my wives
Hid my warriors' beards.

    They took too many liberties,
    Nothing's been the same since that day on the beach.
    And I thought they were gods
    Of the land that I owned,
    When they made me a prince,
    When they crowned me with thorns.

Rene Thomas

CHANSON DE LA LIBERATION
A Blues for Haiti

Sing me a song
and let this song countenance shadows in seas of blood
and with vigilant strokes
paint starlight on signposts of imperialist histories
strumming revolution through kitchens and fields

Our legacy is a circle of wild wind
like the grenadine hips of a fine woman possessed by L'wa
Palpable the light of Toussaint, Dessalines; Aristide...
but come to know the drowning choruses of the unnamed
the children floating down streams of bad water -
away from archipelagos of soft dark bosom

Morning caught us in a raging storm of greenhouse gas
Hurricane chased away sums of pigment and bone
Armed brigades surround and occupy our country
Run tell Uncle Sam that this is not his home
Sing me a freedom song

"There is this rumour of un-watered dawn
of separate land and aqueous sea
A sun that knows no sky-fall
Where the only whirlwind will be me"

Sing me a song.

Kamaria Muntu

SCORPION STING OF MY RHYTHM

Sting of my rhythm arouse dozing minds,
To rise up and arouse the dozing minds
To provoke slumber to life
And stupor to sobriety
I am not addicted to mental slavery.
I have to discard some burden in the journey to my destiny.
Wrongs have to be righted.

Mbizo Charisha

BLACKOLOGY II

Black is my philosophy
Expressed in a black reality
Applying my black methodology
Black a black is I every day levity

I am a Black man
With black blood
Flowing in my vein,
Pumping
Through my heart
Black is the manner
I eat, walk and talk,
Black is a treasured
Possession
Annointing my arms.

Black minded ideas
Projecting black thoughts,
Giving birth to
Black visions.
Black utopia
Black consciousness
My focus unveiling
The black I and I
Seeking the black truths
Entrenched to my black roots

I is the black tree of life
Propagating nurtured
Black fruits.
In my garden
Black roses are in full bloom.

I am the building blocks
Of black foundations
I am the blackness
That brings forth light
Black is in
Never out
Positive
Black stands tall
There's no doubt
Black stands
Predominant

                                        Lloyd Akinsanya

AAAAAAAAAAAAAAAARGHHHH!

AAAAAAAAAAAAAAAArghhhh!---
---bolish all
celebration, commotion,
promotion of the notion
that we are free,
de owner of de plantation
now owns de penitentiary

I hear voices:
A chemical brown voice
blairs out
from behind
a plastic bush:

ASBO
TESCO
GITMO
LET'S GO
BACK TO WORK
BACK TO SCHOOL
NO STOPPING
BUSINESS AS USUAL
– CARRY ON SHOPPING.

Organic green voice
spreads seeds
like
neglected weeds:

aaaaaaaaaaaA-bolish all
co-operation with multi-national corporations,
i-pod, i-phone, i-home, i-clone,
i, i, i… me, me, me, me,
quicker cheaper contracts

cannot bring liberty,
turn off big brother,
see reality c--c--t--v
de owner of de plantation
spells apartheID with ID…

Chemical brown
blairs out
from behind
plastic bush:

HUMAN RIGHTS
HAVE GONE WRONG
POLITICAL MADNESS
HAS GONE CORRECT
SEVEN SEVEN
NINE ELEVEN
DATES WE CANNOT
EASILY FORGET.

Organic green
spreads seeds
like
neglected weeds:

aaaaaaaaaaA-bolish
abomination
of a bomb-making nation.
erase email,
turn Facebook face to a book,
reclaim time and space
that MySpace took,
look up from the gutter,
dim stars of celebrity,

the owner of de plantation
CEO of military…

brown blairs
behind chemical bush:

FREE PRESS
FREE VOTE
FREE MARKET
FREE TRADE
EVERYTHING UNDER CONTROL
DON'T ASK WHERE –
OR HOW – IT'S MADE.

green spreads weeds
neglected seeds:

aaaaaaaaaaaA-bolish de myth
of freedom granted
by philanthropist
free freedom fighting names
of CLR James,
Nkrumah, Nanny, Nehanda and a
thousand Dessalines;
stitch bullet-holes of history
and herstory to see
de owner of de plantation
media monopoly…

brown blairs behind bush:

STICK TO THE CURRICULUM
STAY ON COURSE
TURN TO THE CHAPTER
"ABOLITION

= WILBERFORCE".
DO NOT UPSET THE SPONSORS
NO, IT'S NOT HYPOCRITICAL
FEEL FREE TO SPEAK FREELY
JUST MAKE SURE IT'S NOT
PO-LIT-I-CAL.

green weeds spread seeds:

*aaaaaaaaaaaA-bolish
media monopoly, ID, military,
abolish bomb-making nations,
abolish corporations,
abolish the penitentiary
and – to be truly free,
abolish plantation owners
of de e-k-k-k-onomy.*

Simon Murray

REPARATION SONG

[influenced by Sister Ekua, Brother Kofi Klu
& Robert Nesta Marley]

INTRO: *Wilberforce was the White saviour,*
All Afrikans are dumb di dumb dumb

Old private—companies, yes, they *still* rob i;
      Sold I Wilberwash and "heroes" like William Pitt,
Centuries after they supposedly freed i
We still dealing with destruction of we culture—identities—
institutions
      —society—religions—philosophy—land—peoples—
history—herstory
      and Black inferiority/ White supremacist bull-shit.
But my Haitian brothers and sisters were strong
By repelling the armies of Spain, Napoleon and Blighty.
They died for this generation
Rebelling Triumphantly.

So, Wont you help to bring
      some movement towards long-awaited—much-
needed—deserved
      and necessary freedom? -
'Cause we all need to have:
Reparations dialogue;
Reparations dialogue.

Do not congratulate yourselves for abolition of slavery;
When kkkapitalism still capture we body & minds.
Wo! Pay no tax for atomic weapons or energy,
'Cause all-o-dem-a is just climate crime.
Long must we kill their profits,
Till they stand aside and look? ooh!
Yes, the human race, we're all a part of it:
They got to give back what they took.

Wont you help to bring
Dese first—steps—in—the—process—of—global—justice—
truth—reconciliation—and—
     overstanding—the—complexities—and—legacies—
of— *Maangamizi*
     (the—Afrikan—holocaust—of—chattel—colonial—
and—neo-colonial—enslavement)
     and true freedom? -
'Cause we all need to have:
Reparations dialogue;
Reparations dialogue;
Reparations dialogue.

                                               Simon Murray

THE BRAIN-BURNING

Which part of you is African,
The swarthy skin that oozes desperation?
The black spidery hair that clings to sugar
And begs reparation ,
Only to bring forth ivory tusks
And malversation?
Toil and sweat of an exiguous life
You have not known.
You are an eyeless American,
You were not brought to life in Africa,
In that wild and unruly land that is Africa.
The sylvan glory of America lies at your feet
Yet you cry for Africa,
And deny glorious America.

Your cousins swindled me from Africa,
When they took mine and shoved me to America,
As they stripped off my name and lexeme, put me in stoves,
And cooked my soul to feed theirs,
With carbon-free sugar-cane stilettos.
Yet here, you, their descendant,
Stand demanding the same,
Brain-burning and questioning
And the falsifying of,
The past in the present in the hunt to forget Africa,
As they were to forget Africa and me.

There is no Africa and no me,
No Africa and no me.
'Me' does not exist nor does Africa,
No Africa, No me,
Know Africa, know
me.

Deka Ibrahim

HAITI

Sent on ships with shark-rancorous crews
  That beat human beings
  Until blood bombarded the decks,
  Some Africans were taken to Saint-Dominique.
  Though oppressors lived to destroy joy,
  The stolen, worry-swollen
  Africans in a Caribbean,
  Mephistophelean-ruled land
  Defied tragedy's tide and revivified hope.
Years of lash and gash chattel anguish
  Inspired tears comparable to cloudbursts.
  Within the sorrow
  And wishes for a greater tomorrow,
  Toussaint came to fill dissenters' will.
  His legion's revolt brought their slavery to a halt
  Which removed crazed-with-sin Napoleon.
  Africans turned Haitians
  Defied tragedy's tide and revivified hope.
Raging pages of centuries turned,
  Cain-hateful conflicts burned
  Unveiling text on evil,
  Republic upheaval,
  The inferno emergence of insurgence.
  Haiti felt the hollow hunger
  Stab with fiscal strife's knife,
  Nonetheless, the burden beset Haitians
  Defied tragedy's tide and revivified hope.
Upon their battered habitat,
  Where every being and thing shook
  And took people to disaster-laid graves,
  Haiti's value-engraved resource—
  Courageous will—was saved.
  Again, again Haitians
  Defied tragedy's tide and revivified hope
  With their universe-enormous,

Religious regard,
Defied tragedy's tide and revivified hope
With their every rhythm and limb
Communion dances,
Defied tragedy's tide and revivified hope
With their pulsating,
Disposition-sating songs.
No matter the conflict's length,
Haiti possessed a hero's strength.

Bob McNeil

LONG LINE OF RUNNERS (Lifetime 1)

She ran. She ran until her feet lost focus and her mind found no place to wander. She ran past purpose and reason, through promise and fulfillment. She ran from everything imaginable, but towards nothing. And this ... no, this was not her fault. No one ever told her she came from a long line of runners. Her great, great grand father was a runner ... ran from the Saint Domingue sugar plantation ... left, when it was found out that he had ruined the new, pretty, mulatto chamber maid Master had been eyeing for himself. ... They said he left dust tracks behind him, and all that could be seen was the blinking of heels as each foot descended to kiss the earth and rose-up again to praise the sun. ...They said he almost reached the shores of *Ginen;* that his magical feet had carried him across the waters. ... Said he was almost home again ... almost free again ... almost whole again, when he remembered the seed he had just planted. *How would it grow without a gardener to train the vine?* And if it were a son, *how would he ever be able to stand firm in fertile ground, with missing roots?* So he returned an ear and toe less of a man then when he had left, only to find his garden uprooted; his field stripped barren. ...They had bound her feet before sending her to the market place, with a note that read

"This gal here- ruined and carry lightening in her belly. Keep her ankles shackled at all times to protect future property."

...They said he stayed in the cane fields until harvest time came around. ...Dug his nine toes into the ground and kept his eyes shielded from the sun, from the horizon. Marked and maimed, they all said he'd be a fool to run. But *'wounded'* is not *'dead'* and the blood marching through his veins could not be stilled, ... so on the night the spirits called all of them, he unfastened his soles from the earth, wrapped his feet in dried banana leaf, soaked them in *clarin*, and lit them on fire. With torch in hand and on feet, he ran lighting circles around and through the plantation. ... He ran past shackles and lost lineage, through flesh and limitation, towards home. ... And while his body lay smoldering on a pile of ashes that were once Master and Mistress, somewhere on the other side of the island, lightening struck.

Christine-Jean Blain

COME SEE

Hey cousin come see
visit our undiscovered land
and know media failed to show
Haiti's true glow
Be charmed by our towns so bright and gay
Go on, you, stay one more day
The mountains tell the whole story
of loss, love, rebellion and glory
As birdsong floats from the trees
smell the aroma of our coffee
See now where would you rather be
I see you tapping to that beat
don't hold back get in the street
The carnival has just arrived bet you're glad to be alive
So many dead, yes, and still so many survive,
wait and watch our people thrive
World stop looking at Haiti with eyes of pity

and know we offer more
Though now a part of our great history
this earthquake does not define Haiti
Hey cousin come see.

Sophia Wilson

STILL
(for Haiti)

Is Haiti a page
torn out of a Book
by Someone who thought

This doesn't belong here,
and got angry
at being cheated.

Is Haiti that Book,
sitting limply
in a rain of televised dust

trampled underfoot by bewildered bodies
for whom life and the afterlife
now share one side of a coin

Is Haiti *Atlantis Reloaded* –
death this time by debris; one endless moment
of misfortune? Ta ta. Two hundred thousand

unrequited goodnights, uttered swifter
than the speed of darkness
in a land locked in by History, lit
by pity, lost in the glare of camera lights

II
By the rivers and ruins of Haiti
I sit and sing of restless spirits
rehearsing a re-enactment of 1804;
of *Emancipados* swollen with dreams
of their children pummeling
the stubborn children of *Code Noir*

III
The Book bleeds
but still it holds on to its meaning
Its pages swell with alien pity
but still the characters that inhabit them rise
like the land that threw them off balance

still they sing
still they attempt to dance

even when the music watches
from a safe, safer, safest, distance…

still…

                                              Tolu Ogunlesi

HAITI MORNING COFFEE

A people stolen from their homeland
Shackled to their ruthless, inhumane masters,
Slavery annihilated, mutilated and segregated.
Along came a figure of boldness,
faith and determination to free his people
Touissant L'Overture, savior of the Haitian people,
The chains of slavery unshackled,
colonialism and French rule dead,
The first Black Republic was born.
Vive la révolution! they cried
Liberté! Liberté!

Liberté paid only a passing visit,
a ghost in the depth of the night.
Along came the chains of the new masters
But the Haitian people stood proud
Their souls endured, their bellies stood empty
The world shook their head and said 'Poor Haiti'.

A new visitor appeared, invisible,
Its discord was heard
It outstayed its welcome.
The storm clouds bellowed,
its howls ricocheting over the land
Yelling its torrent upon the people
Bodies lay broken, buried like pharaohs
beneath empty tombs and debris,
Trapped beneath collapsed churches and fallen shacks
Buildings ripped to the ground,
Erasing their history.

The world watched,
Each day the death toll rose and people prayed
Beneath the skin of Haitians, are the souls of survivors
Within the souls of survivors, there is hope
Haiti, my dear, soon you will be watching the world
For little does it know that your time will come
The ravages of nature will soon be at their doors
And it is you
who will be watching us with your morning coffee.

Suzanne Creavalle

PART 2

Misfortune is never invited. And it comes and sits at the table without permission and it eats, leaving nothing but bones.

(Jacques Roumain (1907-1945), Haitian author, ethnologist, political activist. Repr. Éditions Messidor (1992). Antoine in Masters of the Dew, p. 166, Les Éditeurs Français Réunis (1946).)

BREAKING NEWS

Corrugated roofs
Rippling like waves at high tide
Earthquake strikes Haiti

Stephanie L. Kemp

I SAW THE RUBBLE

I saw dying boys in the arms of dead fathers
As flies swarm; vultures in flocks they gather
Some twins found hope brought home by Mrs Sathers*
Still a nation bleeds, with no one left to swathe her

I saw the dead, and I also saw the living
I saw despair, even among the breathing
Crying for relief, that no one is giving
A world too busy, to see the grieving

I saw the rubble, the stacked heaps of corpses
I sigh deep, my mind seeks synopsis
My heart bleeds, Pat* blamed it on the 'Forces'
I heard him, 'A pact made rained the curses'

Blame the woes of Haiti on the sins of Toussaint
Praise the foes of Haiti and call them the saints
Judge for yourself your lack of restraint
If you ever lived your life without a taint

Jeffrey Jaiyeola

Mrs Sathers *Betsy Sathers is a widow who adopted a pair of twins who survived the earthquake*

***Pat** *Pat Robertson, a prominent political spokesman for the Christian right in American politics attributed the woes of Haiti on a pact made with the devil in the quest for freedom*

WHERE ALL MANKIND TREADS

Somewhere along this road all of mankind is
destined to walk. I found myself at a point where
I see a ghostly shadow wondering what is its purpose?
 It gave me two paths.
One where I walk a lonely road,
Or where I continue down the rabbit hole
And see how far I can go
settling my curiosity I go down the rabbit hole
What I saw I will never be prepared for the cries
of the children of mankind were deafening
I begged it to stop but it wouldn't
I wanted to drown my sorrows.
My tears wouldn't stop.
I realized that all creatures of the earth
Meet their faith someday!

Andy Nguyen
(7th **Grader, 12 years old)**

AFTER(the)SHOCK

The earth has shifted,
and wounds have re-opened,
wounds we papered over -
there is nothing to absorb this
new spillage of history.

Hands blistered and bleeding,
you, Toussaint, must be searching,
as I am, through that rubble,
sifting our history,
 for *any* survivors of your revolution.

A grimaced face of pain,
in Port au Prince....again,
I have heard that you, we, are cursed....then
how come we survive?

Toussaint, dream -catcher,
they followed, as you bellowed,
 freedom.

Yolanda M Dean

FOR THE MOTHER AND CHILD

Blood seeped down
into the veins of our Earth

and I held my child and cried

for a mother and child
woke that Tuesday to die.

I held my child and cried
for the mother and child in Haiti;

for the memory of Toussaint,
Dessalines;

for the Haitians never mentioned in the books;
for the Haitian with the monkey on his back.

Pat Robertson (and others), tell me, if you know,
why was the black man's god devil;

why was there a price
for the air you breathe in Haiti.

Blood seeped down
into the veins of our Earth

and I held my child and cried.

Ann Margaret Lim

THE AFTERMATH

Sons and daughters of Senegal lay dead and
dying in the streets of Port Au Prince,
hundreds of thousands of them
smothered, yeah crushed beneath the rubbles,
fragments of magnificent architecture.

The screams of the survivors deafened our ears,
as horrific thunderous sounds
rumbled in the bowel of the earth,
terrifying onlookers, sending them scampering
through the streets, stumbling over the
bodies of loved ones.

Their terrified eyes stare at the world
with arms stretched upward pleading for mercy.
Limbs have been severed, bones crushed and skulls
fractured, faces awash with thick red blood flowing
 freely.

In the quake of 2010
The sons and daughters of Senegal saw lives cancelled,
dreams crushed, hopes die and their future went up in flames.

But out of the devastation and tragedy a more resilient
 people will emerge. They will resurrect, rebound
and rebuild. Until then, let the brothers and sisters
of CARICOM foster, nurture, love and care for them!

Opal Minott

A REAL TRUE NIGHTMARE

    I could hear her yelling, screaming to help her, save her, take her away from this horrible reality. "Help! Help! Help me!" I wasn't sure what was happening but I knew it wasn't right, a sudden shake in the ground is never right. "Someone please, please help!" I tried to urge myself to save her, but the screams pushed me back. All I could think was 'what if I didn't come out alive?' I knew in the eyes of someone else this would have been very selfish but for me it was horror, horror of facing the truth. I prayed to God that the shaking would end sometime soon but it wouldn't. Each second that went by was destroying every good thing I had in life, but I knew I couldn't let this disaster take my mom away. I had to save her, she was the only one I had left in life, without her I was no one. "I'm coming mommy!"

There were only a few things left standing in the house while everything else was buried under the precious pieces of what was once my home. It was very hard to see, dust was everywhere. I couldn't keep my feet on the ground, but I couldn't hold back, I had to do what I had to do.

After a few minutes of searching, I found her, lying on the ground looking at me with her hand reaching out to me so I could take her, "I'm coming mommy" but only the rumbling answered. When I finally reached her I took her lovely hand, but something seemed different, she was cold, pale, and stiff. "Hold on mommy, I'll pull you out." But silence was all that was there, I was the only one pulling. At this point I knew it was the end, life meant nothing anymore, and I knew I had to leave with her. I laid myself next to her and prayed that God would take me, take me to my mother. And finally everything collapsed.

I woke up a few minutes later, realizing it was all a dream. As I rolled over to see if mom was already awake, I knew, to my surprise, it wasn't a dream, it was the real, true nightmare of my life.

Tanya Leon
(9th Grader, 14 years old)

HEARTLESS EARTH

Oh earth,
What spittle
Do you spit back to man?

Visiting your worst quakes
On the poorest west

What rain runs
Your stomach
To vomit rage on women

Crushing souls
With your collapsing soles?

Earth!
Criss-cross cracking
Bold building breaking
Wounded wills weeping

Decimating lives
In a rumble of white bodies
Buried to your strange appetite.

You unearth earth
To eat your heart

HAITI

Sanctuary of Martyrdom
Where flesh mingle with dust

Your pain
Shall be the hand
That shall wipe our many tears to come

Your lost
Shall seed the crushed wombs

With offspring to fight
The earth to come

May your crumbled souls rest
Where stones shall be no more.

Uche Francis Uwadinachi

HAITI
(Haiku Poem)

Oh how heartbreaking
Bodies lie trapped in concrete
Haiti, we will pray

Lucreta La Pierre

THE NAMELESS

Devastating Earthquake hits Haiti
Haiti Lies in Ruins
Grim Search for the Untold Dead

The poorest country
in the western hemisphere,
they repeat like a curse.

Nearly 200,000 may be dead.
See it all on High Definition TV
before falling asleep.

There will be images of the untold dead.
The nameless ones to pity or ignore
depending on how we feel
that night.

Close your eyes and see a girl
in her blue school uniform, bent over her lessons.
Her mother at the stove hums and stirs with a wooden spoon
the milk and sugar to make *douce lait*.

When the earth becomes a wave they both fall
to their knees. They sing *Beni Swa Leternel*
Blessed be the Lord.
Rattling roof, crumbling house, concrete to dust.
Waiting in the dark
for the end of the world.

Beneath the rubble the mother's voice
echoes
until by dawn it is hardly a whisper.
Remember, light a candle for me.

There is always time for a miracle.
Schoolgirl rescued among the ruins.

Narratives of redemption, sell.
The reporter composes a face well practiced,
compassionate concern.
You see, miracles really do happen.
(Cut to commercial.)

They were not always nameless, the untold dead.
For every face the cameras do not capture
there is a name and memories
of murmured songs half-remembered
and sweet milk.

Even the uncounted, the forgotten, the unseen
and unkempt, the ones on rutted roads
shrouded in white with scribbled cardboard signs,
even they have a name.

Remember this, when the show is over
and you
turn away.

Nadine Pinede

CELESTE

What Ope told herself was that the gun was not becoming heavier and that it was not getting more slippery and that she would still be able to use it when the moment arrived. She had no doubt that it would work; she had tested it out on a cockerel that very afternoon. At first she had fired from a few yards and missed entirely. The dark blue metal kicked in her hand like a baby avoiding bath time. It was in the hills, so the report did not bring curious bystanders or police, but it occurred to her that the target was small and she was no marksman.

She caught the fowl and tied it between two reedy trees and moved in close. And fired. There was nothing left of the chicken to eat. Pink pulped flesh, feathers, some bones. Ope regretted the waste.

That was hours ago. Now it was early evening, the sun was less intense and the sounds around her were of a settlement preparing itself for bed. Arguments, pots and pans, children squealing, Tupac Shakur, D'Anjou loudly fucking his new wife and Gran Elise talking in a low tone to Loa that nobody saw or even believed in. Ope was waiting in what passed for a front room in the home she shared with her husband. She sat on his favourite chair facing the door, gun held in two hands with the muzzle pointing at where she hoped his heart would be.

She would not need to be a marksman. His bulk would fill the doorway and he would be framed by the light she had left on in the corridor. She would be hidden by the dimness in the sitting room. She had imagined it over a hundred times since buying the gun. He would come into the house yelling her name, slurring it if he'd had rum, and he would find his way to the sitting room. He'd reach for the light, flick it on and off, but there would be no illumination because Ope had removed the bulb. Then, while he was confused, Ope would pull the trigger. In her mind she would hit him first in the gut and then, as he squealed and begged on the floor and the neighbours hit on the windows and front door, she would shoot him in the head. Bang.

In her head it seemed like that. The reality was that she could not stop shaking. The gun got heavier by the minute and her sweat coated the handle. Thoughts of the Virgin kept coming to her mind but she drove them out. This was not the time for guilt.

Do not get thee behind me, Satan. I need you now.

She wiped the sweat off her forehead and felt pain where she had a bruise. The first blow does not really hurt. It is mostly a flash of light and the bright flare of adrenaline pushing your heart faster. It's the second and third that get you because by then the sense of surprise is gone and you know what you're in for. You are fully in the moment, mindful of the pain. But it fades. You can take a lot more punishment than you think because you simply stop feeling pain after a while.

Bertrand. Lean and cocky, with a killer smile and a constant cigarette. Ope had no chance from the moment he set his gaze on her. There was a direct line from there to countless episodes of stolen love-making (he had a wife back then) to divorce and remarriage, to work as a lorry driver, obesity, boredom and regular beatings.

There was no longer a killer smile, just a killer.

That Bertrand would kill her was beyond doubt. He had fractured her skull just before Christmas. Warm blood had seeped out of her ears.

She had secured the weapon by dispassionately sleeping with one of the gangsters that hung around selling weed. She had let him spill his seed inside her because it did not matter anymore. She would have slept with Baba Legba himself if it meant getting away from Bertrand.

Now. Ope would have to shoot him. What would happen to her afterwards was of no consequence.

Then she could hear a key in the outer lock and all of her muscles tensed at the same time. Her arms became rigid stocks straight out in front of her, the gun joining the two together. Her mouth went dry and the heavy plodding footfall was the only sound she could hear.

'Ope!'

She flinched at that, almost dropped the gun. Careful. Wait for him. He cannot harm you anymore.

'Ope, get over here. I'm hungry!'

He lurched to the kitchen, cursed, then opened the sitting room door. Ope squeezed her eyes shut and fired.

A strange thing: the bang of the gun was not this loud when she had shot the chicken. Bertrand tipped over sideways. Not only that but the house seemed to be bending, folding in on itself. The noise of the gun seemed unending.

The roof caved, fell. A girder hit Bertrand right on the forehead and he dropped stupidly. It became dusty and dark, and the wall pressed down on Ope until she could barely breathe.

In the airless blackness everything was moving. The ground had become a sea of concrete flowing like waves on the beach. There was screaming coming from somewhere and electric sparks broke the gloom for seconds at a time.

Ope blacked out.

When she came to a voice was calling to her, not by name, just calling her. There was sand in her eyes and she could not open them. She coughed and coughed. Hands lifted her, tearing off the skin from her shin. She had wet herself, but that was all right. A splash of water to her face. She opened her eyes.

The street looked like it had been bombed. Power lines were down and cables ran crazy and free. Cars were overturned. Houses were flat or canted to one side. Fires burned, sending smoke into the dark night sky. Bodies of the dead, screams of the dying, cries of the desperate.

Then she remembered, the unending noise of the gun...

'Is this hell?' she asked the man next to her.

'Not yet,' he said. He wore some kind of uniform and his French was formal, out of a textbook. 'But it might be, given time.'

He rushed away and began yelling, going through rubble.

Ope walked around in a daze. An earthquake on this day, of all days.

When the aid workers asked her name she said she was Celeste, and gave a fake address.

She never saw Bertrand again.

Tade Thompson

WAKE UP HAITI!!

I heard about the devastation which hit Haiti,
Saw the images of ruined buildings.
Men and women wondering, stunned
As if their souls had been kicked out of them.
Children, babies, their poor bewildered faces,
Tears, confusion, madness and ultimately grief!
Yes grief, I thought.....
My God! What must it be like?

In those moments I became very human,
Very real and yet simultaneously insignificant,
And here I am,
What can I do?
Feel for them, share in their despair
And ultimate desperation....
Oh yes, I know that feeling......
I think they call it 'loss'

Hmmm ...and I remember that pain.
It tricks you at first into believing
It didn't really happen.
That 'Please God'
It's a dream that I'm soon to awaken from.....
Oh!...... What's that you say?
Reality's maiden whispers,
I'm awake?
The darkness surrounding me is real..?
And everything I love around me has gone?

What's that you say?
You, the sun up there?
You say you will shine for me again?
And melt my pain away?
Oh and you....earth down there...
You say one day you will fruit again?
Your friend, the river, sings the same song,

She says, 'I will not dessert you, be quiet and still!
I stand with my back to the wind, closed eyes.
Envisioning all my tomorrows before me
I hear clear waters creeping up onto the land,
The sun and the river dance around me
Caressing my feet as they leave their fertile gift,
Singing, 'You are strong.....live, breathe, grow....'

Marcia Kay Ellis

HAITI EARTHQUAKE AFTERMATH,
Journal Entries

Titanyen, Thursday Feb 11 . . .

This is where they bury the dead. White cross stands on unmarked graves as backhoe trucks drive back to the city to collect more bones to fill the dusty pits.

More bodies will surely follow.

I fear that Loulou will be one of them.

Port-au-Prince, Saturday, Feb 13 . . .

Rainy season is approaching now. Politicians have been unable to come to an agreement of what they will do with the homeless.

"*Pèp la grangou,*" *dit ma tante,* "*et solèy la ap touye nou !*"[1]

There's no need for money... there's nothing left to buy.

Somerville, Sunday, Feb. 14 . . .

Church feels like a funeral service. And I have been unable to talk to God in three weeks.

"All will turn out for the better!" says my pastor.

I'm not so sure if I believe in that.

Kathuska Jose

---

[1] "The people are hungry," says my aunt, "and the sun is killing us!"

KIJAN M SANTIM
(Creole Version)

Mezanmi peyim pa nan gè,
menm kouri kite l tankou moun ki an afè!

Imilyasyon sa a-a-a !
Ke la nati ba nou an, pi mal ke on gè.

Li pa konn alye, li pa konn enemi, li pa konn atoufè!

Li koupe souf kretyen vivan san gade sou koulè po
ak koulè je yo.

Imilyasyon sa pa konn nasyonalite ,
ran sosyal , klas economic, e-e-e latriye!

Mwen te konn di, no money, no justice an Ayiti,

Men lanati di, money pa money, sa ki peri, peri!

Mwen santi m tankou on pye mapou
ki ap goumen pou rete nan tè,

Men van ak sekkous lanati ap fose l derasine tèt li.

Mwen pa gen pitit, men doulè mwen wè nan je manman pitit,

Fè'm santi ke manze lanati banm on kout manchèt nan vant
mwen!

Se nan tè ya manje soti, se nan tè ya dlo soti,
se nan tè ya sous lavi ye,

Men se menm tè sa-a-a, ki vale zanmi'n, frè 'n,sè'n ,
kouzen'n, tonton'n,matant nou, kouzin nou e-e-e latriye!

Tè a souke, li lage malere, zotobre, kokobe,
doktè, enjenyè, plat atè

Dlo nan jem pa ka sispann koule,
lèm gade timoun ki gen pou viv nan mizè

Mwen rive nan on kafou, mwen wè on ti bebe, mwen bo li,
mwen di li

" On jou nan vi a,
ma rakonte w on ti listwa kite pase douz janvye 2010"

Kenz jou apre tè a te fin souke ,
on bon zanmi' m ki te pèdi manman' l,
voye di mwen :

" Si ou wè wap viv jodia ,
ou mèt konsidere tèt ou kòm on nouvo ne.

Si yo mande w ki laj ou genyen,
pa wont di ke w gen 15 jou."

La vi a rèd men map rete djanm paske ak pasyans Ayiti, va wè trip foumi.*

Erline Vendredi

---

* *Ak pasyans Ayiti, va wè trip foumi (with patience, Ayiti will see ant's intestine): This is a Haitian creole proverb that has no English substitute but it means that if we are persistent and patient, we might be able to see the impossible with our eyes.

KIJAN M SANTIM - How I am feeling
(Loose English Translation)

My friends, my country is not at war, but I ran away from it like someone who is in trouble
This humiliation that nature has imposed
on us is worse than war
It does not know allies, enemies, or crooks
It does not discriminate on skin colour, colour of eys, nationality or class
I used to say, no money, no justice in Haiti
But nature says, money or no money, those that died, died.
I feel like a mapou tree (Myrsine) fighting to stay in the soil
But the wind and the tremor of nature is forcing it to uproot
The pain I see in the eyes of mothers
Leaves a stabbing pain in my womb
Food, water come from the earth,
and the earth is the source of life
But it is the same earth that swallowed our friends, our brothers, our sisters, our cousins, our uncles, our aunts
The earth shook, and it dropped poor, powerful folks, handicapped, doctors, engineers flat on the ground.

My tears will not stop when I see the children

I arrived at a crossroad, I saw a baby, I kiss him and told him;
'One day in life, I will tell you a story about something that happened on January 12th 2010'.

Fifteen days after the earthquake, a best friend of mine who had lost his mom sent me a message saying:
" If you are alive today, you can consider yourself a new-born, if you are asked for your age, don't be ashamed to say that you are 15 days old."

The pain is tough but I am staying strong because with patience, Haiti will see ant's intestine.

Erline Vendredi

HOPE FOR HAITI

In the helpless aftermath of the rumble
Trash-trample of finite flesh, equatorial
Upheave, the creak crinkle and crackling
Of burdened belly; In her womb seismic
This foetus ensafed trembling others
Aborted by a quickening tomb...
Within our grim fluttering silence
Frustrated-after claps, man-less limbs, shocked
Trapped cries of voices bloody imperfect
... Blank eyes-land lights won't wake after
This quake to grovel with gory fingers
Thru grief's rubble from never 'til forever!
After the crumble of bones and trowelled stones
Aghast O's and Ahh-mens definitions
Of disaster-prone my bleeding pen tongue
Lurid tales tell rescues of desperate men
Fighting for survival in fields of tents
... Most High now all laud thy mercy
From dust build up... let there be hope for Haiti!

Fitzroy Cole

REQUIEM FOR HAITI

The rich green of grass and emerald paired
Parrots pipe t(h)rill flock and flutter storm stilled ears
(Aired at six-o-three a-men
Another quake quacked Haiti again!)... Looking
Legs-less black-brown bodies with laundry-pegs
Cling cloud clutter power-cables overhead
(Oh mourning solemnic) this drooping line
Of nightingales in silent requiem
Full-feathered monument (un-pooping, staid)
To fresh-remembered dread!

Fitzroy Cole

NOTHING MAKES SENSE ANYMORE

Nothing makes sense anymore, my sister.
The dead words in my mouth can't say how I feel
And forgive me, Lord, but it hurts when I kneel.
For they say the age of miracles is over,
But when will the horrors end so that we can heal?

Nothing makes sense anymore, my sister.
Mountains of cement and rebar have buried your lover,
His smile greeted you at five every day when you shared a meal,
But breath left your body when you saw the Citadel reel.
Nothing makes sense anymore, my sister.

Geoffrey Philp

WHY ME?

Me sister.

Her lad.

Me best mate.

His dad.

Our baby.
Our baby.
Our baby.

Me father.

Me nan.
Me grandad.

Me mam.

Our baby.
Our baby.
Our baby.

Me brother.

His wife.

Me daughters.

My wife.

With our baby.
Our baby.
Our baby.

Tony Walsh

THE NATURAL ORDER OF THINGS

Behind the graveyard
A new home etched in concrete
Father buries son

Stephanie Kemp

EARTH TREMBLING

Trembling earth and fallen buildings
A metaphor for a humanity that has collapsed from within
Third world country held at mercy by Western Sin
Sinful activities that endorse the poor man's sufferings
Unable to see beyond the cameraman's lens
The whole world is made to spectate
Tales of looting get magnified
One is quickly made to realize
That the purpose here
Is not to donate
But to portray
The black man as criminal and deranged
An animal that cannot be tamed
Relentless in their quest
Humanitarian causes get spun with finesse
The subliminals are forever there
The message is still clear
Although they supposedly care for the mothers and sons
A brief moment of reflection
Shall free your mind from submission
Disguised as good Samaritans
The lighter skinned Man
Shall descend on their land
And restore civilization
A story often told
In times of colonization
But what can you do when Evil prevails
And when voodoo type spells
Got us surviving in this living type hell
Where the flames are still scorching
The Aftermath is still dawning
Two months down the line
And we shall still be yawning
Embracing our morning tea
As we switch on the news

And get our glimpse of reality
But not to worry
Haiti is now a distant memory
Similar to Katrina
The hurricane has erased all imagery
No more accountability
No more brotherly love
No more feelings of solidarity…
Earth trembling, buildings falling
A mirror image of a collapsed humanity.

Alexander Thanni

HAITI

How to rebuild Haiti
A land lost of 200 year history
Such death and loss paralyses me
How can this be?

A land that has defeated slavery
Fought and gained freedom, no longer a colony
Independence, now just a memory
How can this be?

Mother Nature acts out of hand
Causing destruction to their land
Is this part of a bigger plan?
How can this be?

Loved ones lost in the blink of an eye
Survivors stand too stunned to cry
Mothers in labour no time to be shy
How can it be?

How to rebuild Haiti
A land once warm, joyous and free
Will too this now fade into just a memory?
How can this be?

Akilah Moseley

HAITI LOST

I see a flow of tragedy
Wasting humanity
I see pain and agony
Simple reality
Lord of the sympathy
Is calm such a mystery?
Don't let their ethnicity
Turn into history.

Blessed from all, from you and me
Land of the Haiti
We'll give you power to see
The path of victory
Don't act trapped like a weed
Don't hold back, just proceed
Both what is and what will be
You shall be free.

**Acquaye McCalman
(16 years old)**

SOON

I have poured
    A bucket of fresh tears
    On that young grave
For the gritty sand to be softened....

Women have onto dust bath
Rolling in broken towns
    Sagging their satins
    And left beings
In earthling clay of agony

Toddling teens
Became scenes, starved
To their tongues and jaws
In anthem of the dark days

We watch, wailing, waiting, wanting
To see the earth quiver
And let the pathetic air souse
Touching the navel of that
Limb tit in the pit

The louder the orphan's anguish
The lower the sky set silence

That eclipse our nearest
Shadows, sending us ALL
Back home

In a clumsy match queue of geese
Treading back to their lease to sleep
Unanswered

Soaking our swollen eyes
In tears ...through the night
Dawn waits earnestly

Morning soon shall come to take
Mourning far, far
Away from Haiti.

                              Uche Francis Uwadinachi

PART 3

For oft from the darkness of hearts and lives
Come songs that brim with joy and light,
As out of the gloom of the cypress grove
The mocking-bird sings at night.

> *From The Lesson by Paul Laurence*
> *Dunbar (1872 – 1906)*
> *Courtesy of Poets' Corner*
> *(<http://theotherpages/poems/>)*

A LIME JEWEL

A little girl,
a gold-wrapped
bonbon damp in
her cherry-skinned fist,
the mellow swirl
of another, whirling
in her mouth.
Lime.
Mango.
Banana.
Papaya.
The fruit of
the black soil
caught in a jewel of sugar.

Beneath her powdered feet,
rubble,
beneath the rubble,
pitted tarmac,
asleep beneath the tarmac,
black Jacobins.

She sucks,
They dream,
She appraises,
They dream,
She weeps,
They dream.

She tints the world with the lime of her bonbon.
Bitter. Sweet.
Wasteland melting into dreamland,
Cold, crystalline and curiously lit.

The light of Haiti,
once filtered

by palm fronds,
then cutlassed
by sugar cane,
is now caught tight
in a lime jewel.

A symphony of blood
gushes in her,
her skin is the shroud
of saints,
dreams are breathed out of the earth,
and into her,
Cold, crystalline and curiously lit.

Nadifa Mohamed

11 DAYS AFTER THE QUAKE

Blood seeps through
the belly of creaking wood.
Water laps like rabid dogs.
There's no escape!
"Riverboat people"
hold up their dusty bodies
and distant stares,
overloaded with aches.
The world shouts,
"Help is on its way!"

Prayers ring out,
as shockwaves shatter.
A ferry rocks full of worry.
Trembling hands tap Bibles.
Where there's a will,
there's a way.
Sandy toys and water pails are
clutched in the fade of the wind,

fused to the nightmare
of broken bones,
amid the ruins, kith and kin
are pinned by pylons.
The dead are piled up
like crash test dummies,
plunging from metal claws
to gapping adders in the earth.
The world shouts,
"Help is on its way!"

Sad people do not leave this
ruptured turf
where forefathers fought
so bravely to harness.
Where there's a will,
there's a way.

Before, the world ignored
your grueling agony and
longing for better things to come.
You were seen as a scratch on the map,
a graze in the western hemisphere.
Now you live in tent cities
where rainbow-coloured sheets
shield not against disease.
Where are the cures to ease this nagging pain?

The world shouts, "Help is on its way!"
Some say, you should ride back
to your crumbling dwellings
in the rusty, multi-coloured buses,
baking in the Haiti sun.
Where there's a will,
there's a way.
In your faintness and sickness,
claim your rights
to rebuild your culture
and leave not your heritage
to unknowing hands.
The world shouts,
"Help is on its way!"

Sip water from the UNICEF
pools of plastic-like bladders,
with sore hands scoop up grains of rice
the fleeing trucks scatter,
far and wide babies wail
for milk and dead mothers

on fly flooded streets where corpses lie,
rotting in the sear of the sun.
The world shouts,
"Help is on its way!"

Amongst the maggots and mould,
you can rise again,
strong and dignified.
Let the memory of loss
lift weary legs to stand
and broken hearts to mend.
Where there's a will,
there's a way.
Sift the airborne torment,
oozing its caustic reek,
and fight to be recognised, counted.
The world shouts,
"Help is on its way!"

Sing psalms to recall the smiles
and joys of the fallen ones
whose remains lie tangled
in the pit of silence.
Your bloodline is resilient!
Feel outside the box, heal.
Independence will come again!
Where there's a will,
 there's a way.
The world shouts, "Help is on its way!"

            Maroula Blades

RISING OF THE MORNING SUN

One hand rests on her womb
Questioning
The other hand latches onto the wind, a wind that is
Flying on the hopes of a foreign promise
And just watching this, my spirit feels novice, my hands feel
Empty
When I'm reaching but can't touch the homeless, humbled
and shamed because my home holds
Plenty
Plenty of possibilities for every square foot of hardwood,
holes, and rugs
While my sister searches for pulses on wrists
with open veins praying for drugs
To calm the infection
Rooted in this seamless search for direction
In a frozen snapshot of time where both east and west
offer no protection
Just the lunar eclipse of helicopters dropping
shrink-wrapped manna from the skies
The depth of her pain cannot be wrapped around
language, so instead she screams out through
Her eyes
Yet there is a stirring like a whirling in her spirit
that will rise
As sure as the rising of the morning sun
She is strong like each braid on her head –each strand is
Symbolic and
Evidence of the strength
That is destined to break out into a
Tribal revival
dance
What a romance, this marriage of
Purpose and Pain
What a beautiful storm when each drop of rain
Seeps deep beneath the crevices of concrete

to the lips of those beneath the earth
alive
The same thunder that brings the doubt,
it brings the water
To survive
It rinses the questions, and conceives more questions
It's all heartache in her eyes
Yet there is a stirring in her spirit that will rise
As sure as the rising of the morning
Sun.

Stacey Lois Howard

LIFE

Life is the scaffolding web of humanity,
When one falls, we rebuild.
Life is the flow of a raging river;
We must move steady,
Life is as the sun rises,
Then sets;
So must we.
Life: is it a gift,
A road of suffering?
If life is not fair, what is?
Life is as a roller coaster;
It has ups and downs.
No matter what life has been chosen for you,
Hope,
Keeps us together.

Nick Falconer
(7th Grader, 12 years old)

A PRAYER FOR HAITI

The earth has divorced you cruelly
At the expense of losing your home,
Vanished in a flash
With many of your beloved children,
The whispering wind is giving you a strong message,
Not to be discouraged.
Look up to the One
Whose creative power
Can rebuild and restore your dignity.
May He hear your cry and prayer.

              Esther Ackah

SINGING OUR OWN SONG

I sway uncontrollably. The drumming pounds like my heart, beating its rhythmic lifeblood through my veins and arteries; each thump a wakeup call to me, yelling for my ancestral lineage, my history to make itself known; for me to know, to feel, to be. I dance in the middle of a clearing, amongst a group of drummers sitting in a rough circle. To one side the elders chant a song of a thousand years or more. Children just before them match our every move. Behind their shaking bodies reaching for the blue-black sky, is Pic la Selle, its craggy blackness outlined, separating the Earth from the Cosmos.

As if there is a need to join the musical harmony, I can hear crickets chirping, creating their own song, singing their own tune; a precursor for all the other night noises to join in. The leaves in the trees rustle, adding their divined response as they whisper about their journey, quietly singing their song. Everywhere there's a vibration. Everything lost in nature's magnificent mind.

But I am not alone, lost in this blissfulness. Dressed in colourful, flowing *baddahs* our bare feet kick dust clouds, into our nostrils, onto our clothes fabric, all over our skin; our drummer's hands move in unison, whilst our feet cause more powdery mayhem. Men and women, pitch and roll, dip and dally, moving to the earth-shattering throbs.

Eventually my mind is lost in the pulsations and I see the images of people in their thousands, their hands chapped and bloodied from lifting large mounds of concrete blocks. Like ants devouring morsels of sweet food, they scrabble about the dusty dunes, digging however, with whatever they can lay their hands on.

Then I hear a song. I can hear them singing.

It's the same song we are moving to. It was the same song we sang when we rebelled against those slave masters who treated us as sub-humans; who beat, raped, pillaged, murdered and mutilated our children, mothers, fathers, aunties, uncles, sons and daughters. The same song we sang when we burnt the sugar cane fields to the ground. From Exuma in Bahamas, Matanzas in Cuba, Colihaut in Dominica, Berbice in Guyana, Morant Bay in Jamaica to Bloody Bay in Trinidad.

It was the very same song.

As I bopped, I could hear the harmonious words while shovels, mechanical diggers and any other implement strike solid masonry. Stupefied in my trancelike movements, I can hear the sadness at the loss of those who have perished in the Earth's uneasiness and the wails of those now with the Ancestors. And yet my ears pick the distinct sounds of determination garnered from those same Ancestors, their legacy of coming through hardship and persecution, what it meant to be here with all the devastation, to know we are bowed but not defeated.

I see their blood spilt through violence and pain, pushing my dancing into a flurry. My insides tremble, my organs are alive; I feel the unseen consciousness filling me, its energy flowing through me, touching us all as we dance.

Our solemn dance of pain. Our dance of victory against tyranny and hate. Our mad dance of success, of our freedom.

My feet ached, my head hammered. I am not the only one and I know I can't ask, there is too much at stake. Looking at the children dancing away, I smiled at the legacy we continued and knew we would rise again. Our country would be great. Our nation will be great. Once again.

I chant. I hum. I am singing the same song.

Kwame MA McPherson

MY

My Haiti was once a beautiful place
now all is left is a people devastated
with more hunger and despair
I will pray for you, I will share my
abundance with you
know that I love you, know that I will
keep you in my heart always, know that
the world will come to your aid
The world overheard your cries my
beautiful Haiti, your despair will turn
into hope, your tears will be wiped
away
do not give up, after the many deluges,
the time has come for many colorful
rainbows!

HAITI

Nicole Weaver

CATCHING THE TAP-TAP TO CAYES-DE-JACMEL

Lucien pulls at bits of broken wood, hoping to hear the hard rattle of plastic. He found a soft drink here before, and some chocolate. But that was a long time ago now. Two, three days? He's been down here now, he doesn't know how long. How do you tell when there's no light and your phone battery is flat? Just inches away, there could be more food or drink that he hasn't yet found. Best keep searching. No use being all skin and bones when they finally pull him out of here.

Lucien wonders how many other buildings toppled in the quake. He wouldn't be surprised if this was the only one. It was one of the older buildings in the neighbourhood, and it's not like his boss invested very much in maintenance: on a windy day, the place had always looked about ready to fall down.

He hears a tapping from off to his left.

"You still hanging on there, Luc?"

The old woman, Agnes, her voice a hoarse whisper.

"Oh yes, I'm not going anywhere."

Each of them is trapped in a separate air pocket. He's never seen her, but since it happened he's come to know her voice. Agnes was watching a film when the building came down. Lucien was starting the late shift, and was chalking up next week's schedule on the blackboard – a weekly task he likes better than his real job, which is selling tickets.

"You've been quiet," she says. "They've all been quiet awhile."

The first day, Agnes told him she could hear five or six people tapping.

"They're resting," Lucien says. "Keeping their strength up for when we get out of here."

She doesn't mention the ugly sweet smell that seeps in and mingles with the stale dusty air. Nor does he. Neither of them wants to think about that.

He knows he can't reach the old lady but to cheer

her up he adds: "If I find more bon-bons, Agnes, I'll split them with you, I promise."

"I'll hold you to that," she says.

And he knows he's made her smile.

#

The smile in her voice reminds him of his mama. It's a long time since he spoke with Mama. Months now. Lucien misses her voice. When he was little, after his father left, she often talked with him at night until he fell asleep.

If he closes his eyes, it's like there is no broken cinema on top of him. No, he's standing in the sunlight outside Mama's house. Breathing in fresh air. When all this is done, if he walks away from this, he's going home...

He stops himself.

Not if. When. *When* he gets out of here.

Mama's doing fine, he knows it. In the village outside Cayes-de-Jacmel where she lives, the buildings are small and light, with no concrete floors to fall on people and trap them. Home is only a single storey house. Besides, there's the timing: this quake came late in the afternoon, at the start of his evening shift. Mama's always out and about at that time of day feeding hens or driving goats to their pen. The worst that could have happened to her is she fell over and picked herself up again.

Mama's a strong woman. The night the hurricane blew the roof off, she made all the children huddle together in the kitchen while the wind howled around them, little Rousseline crying and hanging on to her teddybear to stop it from blowing away. Before dawn the wind calmed and they slept. When they woke, Mama was gone.

Soon, though, they heard her voice, from outside: "Luc, Zach – come quick and help me with this."

She had found the tin roof in some trees nearby and dragged it home single-handed. She battered the corrugated metal into shape and together they set it back on the walls, weighting it down with heavier stones than before. That's how strong Mama is.

\#

Lucien finds no more chocolate, but in this darkness a glimpse of the outside world is better than any sweet. He feels stronger.

When all this is over he's going to get out of this damned ugly-beautiful city. It mesmerised him when he first got here: the hustle of so many people like a hundred market days jammed together – far too many people for him to ever know all their names and remember their stories like he did back home. But now that he's been here a few months, Lucien knows that Port-au-Prince and Cité Soleil are not so special as they seemed from far away. Lucien also knows that if he leaves now he won't be driving home behind the wheel of a four-by-four like he'd planned. That would have made Mama extra proud, because she loves to tell people how well her sons are doing. But he sees now that it would have taken him years, maybe more years than she has to spare. And he knows she'll be pleased to see him just as he is. That's good enough for him.

\#

When Lucien told Mama he was going to the city, she cussed him for two days solid. She barely spoke to him the day before he left, but the next day she got up before dawn, made him breakfast and sat and watched him eat it. She even walked to town with him, which surprised him - the only time she ever left the house that early was to tend to her animals.

He was sorry to drag her uptown so early, but he had to be there in good time in case the tap-tap went. If enough people wanted to leave, the bus would be gone by seven thirty. If not, the driver would sit in the minibus smoking cigarettes until he'd sold all the seats he needed to cover his petrol, then take to the road in the hope of adding enough passengers along the way to take him into profit.

He was lucky. The tap-tap was nearly full when he got there. Only after he paid and took his seat did Mama reach in through the opening to take his hand, and say: "I'm worried you'll be lost to us, Luc. I never once heard from your papa after he left for Cité Soleil."

"I'm not like Papa. You won't get shut of me that easy." He leaned out of the window, kissed her, and handed her his mobile phone. "Listen, Mama, I'm going to need a new phone – take this, and I'll call you tonight, OK?"

She smiled as the brightly coloured bus moved away.

The tap-tap climbed noisily up the steep hill that overlooked the caye, and Lucien felt dizzy when he glanced down a few minutes later. From up here you couldn't see their home – it was hidden by the leaves of banana trees. Closer to town the long stretch of white sand was interrupted by fishermen's huts, a wooden jetty, boats. At the place where the sealed road made a loop and came back, a few buildings stood out: the market, the petrol station, the church. The small crowd gathered at the bus stop had mostly scattered, but Mama was still there. He could see her bright pink dress, the pink scarf she was waving.

He almost told the driver to stop then, and got out and went back. But he didn't. He just leaned out of the open window and waved. He called her every night from Port-au-Prince until his old phone stopped working.

#

Lucien pictures himself telling his boss he has to quit. Then he laughs at very the idea that he needs to quit, because this decision has so clearly been made for him – after all, the cinema's lying in pieces all around and on top of him. And who knows what has happened to his boss? Even if he wanted his job back, he couldn't have it.

Soon as they get him out of here, he's catching the tap-tap to Cayes-de-Jacmel. He pictures the homecoming feast Mama will lay out to celebrate, ranged along the bench in the backyard: fresh fish cooked in banana leaves, rice, fruit... Everyone will be there, all of their neighbours, old Ernesto with his guitar and a song, and his dazzling smile. It will be like a wedding without going to church. And he is going to dance.

#

When Lucien wakes up again, he is cold. His legs are stiff and the one that has been hurting him feels numb.

He taps the wall but no one answers, not even Agnes, and for the first time he feels nervous. His grandma told him before she passed away how she'd seen the blinding white light that comes to people when their souls leave their bodies. He remembers her telling him about the light, at the hospital a few days before she died. She fought the light off that first time, but it came back for her. This is what he's thinking when he sees the white light coming for him.

A physical fear wells up from deep within his body. Lucien shuts his eyes and turns his head away, still fighting. He will not, he must not, see this light. This light is for the dead people – not for him. He wants to live.

Tap-tap.

"You see it?" Agnes's cracked whisper takes him by surprise. "You see that light?"

He really thought the old woman was gone this time. Maybe she *has* gone, and she's coming back to fetch him? Then Lucien grins as suddenly it all makes perfect sense. The world is not ending, it's beginning again.

"Do I see the light? Yes, I see it. And it's beautiful."

"You were right," Agnes says, jubilant. "We are getting out of here."

Lane Ashfeldt

Afternote
The 'tap-tap' is a local name for a kind of private/public bus in Haiti, like this one in the hills near Jacmel. People tap on the bus to get on or off, hence the name. Tap-taps are painted in bright colours and carry the name of their driver/owner over the windscreen.

SOMETHING OF AN APOLOGY

The handmade quilt my grandmother gave me
wraps around my body like
a caterpillar's cocoon
as I watch flashing image[s] of broken
buildings on television.
In the images painted by light
I see people crawling out of dark spaces
their bodies, faces dusted in white debris,
but they are emerging, finally, into
the consciousness of the world
after days (years) of being buried
in the rubble.
Concrete crumbles around their bodies
and their lives like the feta cheese
I ate on my salad this afternoon.
I always knew they were there
but I didn't want to watch the real-life
drama of their poverty
preferring instead to belly-laugh
at the unreality of a laugh-tracked sitcom.
As I sit atop my Memoryfoam
unable to forget my own complicity
I hit mute just when
the man speaks of the
numbers of the dead.
Reaching for my cell phone
I know $10 is not nearly enough;
My cable bill is 120.

RaShell R. Smith-Spears

RISE UP HAITI

Rise up Haiti
From the mud
From the rubble
From the dust and ashes
rise up from the blood

Through the trouble torment and strife I see black hands,
clenched fists rise

Rise up Haiti

The lone child who has lost his mother,
cry not, but find your sisters and brothers and rise.
And know that as you rise, you shine.
You have overcome the heartache before,
you have overcome the bloodshed before...
And as you rise, smile, because we rise with you.
African heart far from the motherland,
Rise, though you feel you can't,
Rise, Rise, Rise.

Phil Gregory

RISE UP HAITI
Surgir Haiti
(French version)

Surgir Haiti,
De la boue
Des décombres
De la poussière et les Ases
lever à partir du sang

Grâce à la peine de tourments et de luttes, je vois les mains noires, la montée poings fermés

surgir Haïti

L'enfant solitaire qui a perdu sa mère, pleure pas, mais trouvent vos sœurs et frères et l'élévation.
Et sachez que, comme vous vous levez, vous rayonnez.
Vous avez vaincu le chagrin d'amour avant, vous avez vaincu le bain de sang avant le ...
Et comme vous vous levez, le sourire, parce que nous nous élevons avec vous, le coeur d'Afrique loin de la patrie.
Levez-vous, si vous vous sentez cant
surgir surgir surgir

Phil Gregory

SURVIVOR
(To Evans Monsignac and all survivors of the Haiti earthquake)

A big bang
This time not to create
But raze
It wasn't like a beginning but an end
Hope that had defied the misery of these slums
Looks set to be subdued by this Armageddon
"This must be hell... my punishment"
A punishment for being poor?

It was a 27 day eternity
Hemmed in by rocks, screaming and then silence and the smell of death
Traumatised, malnourished, emaciated, dehydrated, twisted and wounded
Abraham must have had mercy
Permitting Lazarus to dip his finger in water from the sewer
And cool his tongue
Amidst the horror something remained
That which sustained his troubled ancestors
That which defied the rage of dictators
That which defied the poverty of this land
That which appeared in different forms: God, snake or man
That which brought Salvation
And leads the way to the Land of the Free.
Hope.

Olufemi Amao

ODE TO HAITI

Island of gold, once happy and free,
Smooth yellow sand, sweeping blue sea.
Rebellious symbol of liberty,
Haiti.

Curious Westerners came to teef out your wealth,
Beat, punished, abused your health.
Stealing your riches for themselves;
Sins of the past, Haiti.

Explorers came and raped your land,
Slave blood mixing with the sand.
You worked and cried, escaped and ran,
Your spirit intact, brave Haiti.

They left your country, a shell of its former glory
A sad middle part to a melancholy story
Where, oh where do we go from here?
Haiti, tell me, Haiti.

A shooting star dragged down to earth,
The beautiful place of abolition's birth.
Freedom's child is one you nursed:
We love you dearly, Haiti.

A trailblazer in so many ways,
Over the years made poor, but in a matter of days,
Your country's heart was set ablaze,
Poorest, richest, Haiti.

And to think that while I'm nyamming meat
Haitian children starve in the streets.
Families dead, hope destroyed and nothing to eat,
We pray for you, Haiti.

Nations who enslaved you endeavoured to save
Your dignity, your people, so they gave
Back some of the money they made from your slaves.
A kick when you're down, Haiti.

But in your barren land lies a seed of hope,
Your fighting spirit is still alive.
Will you break? Fall down? Give up? Nope,
With God's grace, Haiti, *survive*.

Georgiana Jackson-Callen
(15 years old)

THE RIPENED FAITH

The ripened faith, the resting grace;
Has it travelled with careworn pace.
He told of the days of the wild
The earth that was stepped on by a child.
Beheld by the burning cyclopean moon;
Modest arms lashed, making mountains of seas,
The drenched dirt to trees

As he walked, with tiny steps uncertain,
Smiling, grabbing at hills, striking at rivers
As if they were toys

As he swayed and fell on forests
The new rivers took his laughter
To places farther and farther.
He went after,
For he had played his game
For it was time to sleep
And he left his toys behind.

Plead the symbols of fortune
Let sleep the rivers of fortitude
For the fort of the night is closing
Laments the greasy layers of solitude
Let loose pleated misfortune
Hither went the amulets
Fetch them whence they are
Arrived at the hour of need
Forces gathered at the doors seem formidable
Arm the men with spears and attitudes
Arm the men with life and hope.

Nash Colundalur

HAITI STRONG

Bewildered yet humble,
faith subsumes Haiti.
Life still exhaled
a burning light
against the rubble.
Lions
Children, brothers
Sisters, mothers
faith empowers,
flowers.
Strong Haiti,
keep strong.

Margaret Danquah

SANKOFA
"se wo were fin a wosan kefa a yenki"

Come together I people
Yeed the ancestors' call,
Wait not till our
Backs are against the wall,
'Tis time to retrace our steps
Return an' fetch,
Revisit the ancient rites
Of Kemit,
Retrace the forgotten path
An' pick up where we have
Left off,
Let's move to the future by
Taking from our past,
Mend and reconcile where
Things have fallen apart.

UMOJA I people
Yeed the ancestors' calling,
It's time for unity,
It's every man's duty
To know where he stands,
Remember African man
Can't give away a continent
For an island,
Melanin man
Move away from
The sinking sand,
Nubians in the Diaspora
Aluta Continua.

Africa awaits its creators
Repatriating from
Distant shores and borders,
Woman, man and children
Unto Itiopia stretch forth I n I hands,

Together in communal bond
One for all, all for one
That's our song
Affirmations of the Nubian
It's a liberation procession,
Dubbing redemption songs
No more singing by the rivers
Of Babylon.

Forward proceed
Hailing the man of the East
With his children and queen,
Supreme beings reunited
Through the doors of no return
I'm making my entrance
Now for sure fire got to burn
Nyabinghi purification,

Blacks in the diaspora
Where you at
Move from the white man's table,
Stop, stoop and squat
Time to get back to Black,
Take a stance embrace
The mother land,
With all her problems
We are her solutions,
She awaits her creators
Carried beyond the shores
Of Europe and the Americas.

Sankofa here I come
Through the door of no return
Reclaiming the I n I
Freeing my mind

From the Uncle Tom mentality
I've seek, found and re-instated
My lost identity.

Lloyd Akinsanya

WAKE UP TO HAITI!

Look at Haiti and what do you see?
A trashed old land next to the sea

People struggling to get by
Babies crying as if they're going to die

Nobody knows what's going to happen
If they're going to eat or go to heaven

And yet we're all proud of ourselves because we gave money
But don't we realise it won't feed the many

So from this day let's show some appreciation
For what we have is more than this brave nation.

Jai Ellis-Crook
(10 years old)

HAITI MY GENERATION

Haiti, Haiti, Haiti

Sorrow stole the heart of the land
with its shameless wings
Lungs of the east suffocating under the wings of sorrow
South heaving with heavy smell
of sweat and crowded bitterness
The West drunk with blood of the gumless,
born children and some unborn
The north intoxicated in tears
washing wounded moon and hearts

Death whispered terror in the marrow of this land
the land became death, the land groaned in agony,
lungs of the earth heaved, death of the beloved

Deathly wings flapping down green bushes,
love eaten by darkness

Babies buried themselves,
mothers went way in madness, smiling love
Seekers of divine run buzzing in bee-hive collective
Singing eulogies and laments in this perspective
Haiti Haiti Haiti

Don't go to bed, with tears burning your tender heart
And with sweat of grief scrawling
on your trembling thighs
Darkness is swallowed by light
Energetic sun spears spring eastwards
Heaven smiling to souls
that went unwilling and unknowing

Crimeless generation,
when nature calls even kings whimper.
Fire does not burn one bush, every time
I will sing you a song , a eulogy, crimeless generation
I will sing you until the tongue of the moon kisses the
tender skin of your nights
until Sahara weeps tears of water
until the fingers of the sun caress the dry belly of
Kalahari.

Drink cups of hope with delight
Drink mugs of peace with hope
Light the candle lights, listening to silent freedom coming
Whispering moments of redemption
Haiti, crimeless generation
I am on your lap, from somberness to the day when
Laughter laugh again
To the dawn when flowers bloom their bloom again
Smiles triumph shadows
Haiti, my generation,
I lick your bitter tears
with my metaphors of love
drink your sweet sweat with the tongue of my syntax.

Mbizo Chirasha

DOES LIFE HAVE A PURPOSE?

Does Life Have A Purpose?
After all there is pain,
People crying,
There are wars,
People dying.

Does Life Have A Purpose?
There is corruption,
Single mothers,
Homeless beggars,
No - one bothers.

Life Does Have A Purpose.
To forgive and forget,
To support each other's needs,
To appreciate each other's differences,
To listen to each other's pleas.
We need to help each other,
Even though some are out of range,
If we all strive side by side,
Together we can make a change.

David Larbi
(12 years old)

HE

Look into my future, what do you see?
Money in my palms, what about he?
He in Haiti, whose future is unclear,
He, whose path is not straight.

Look into my eyes what do you see?
A happy girl, yeah that's me,
What about he, whose eyes are sad and sunken,
He, traumatised by the disaster.

Compare us both then you will see,
Compared to him, I am the luckier one,
While he whose future is unclear and,
He whose eyes are sad and sunken in,
Still has hope,
Hope to become a better person.

Abigail Perry Duah
(11 years old)

I KNOW THAT IT MAY HURT

I know that it may hurt to know
There are families and children who came into this world
To be mistreated and taken in the care of the wrong hands

I know that it may hurt to know
The hope and love that your family was holding on to
Has been demolished and destroyed to the floor

I know the feeling of worry,
Wondering are they ok, have they survived,
Will they live to sing another song or read another book,
Or pray another prayer or eat another meal?

I know it hurts to wonder
Will these kids get a chance to pursue a dream,
Welcome a new life or a talent or help another praying hand
That needs a hand to hold the puddle of their tears?

I know that it may hurt to know
That if there was a spot for talent it would be theirs,
If there was a place in ones heart it would be theirs,
If there was a hole in love and a cure for pain they would fill that hole.

I know that it may hurt,
God knows that it hurts but he moves in many shapes and sizes
And he knows the good in their heart and yours.

I know it may hurt to know
The words you have to share can't save the pain of families
Suffering for a better life.

I know that it may hurt to know
When they get up in the morning they have to question them selves
Are we coming or going

If they're in good hands or bad hands
If they will survive one more day to tell their families they love them
No matter what happens nothing will tear them apart.

LaTrell Johnson
(10th Grader, 15 years old)

TRUE SPIRIT

The sun shines brightly on a damaged land,
Where villagers carry on as much as they can,
Houses crushed to rubble,
Families blown apart,
How can Mother Nature take such a part?
In a time of adversity,
The true Haiti spirit shines on,
Like the sun beaming down on them,
They will remain strong,
While the earth may shake and buildings may fall,
One thing is for sure,
Haiti's spirit never will.

                                            Kathy Cakebread

SERPENT AND THE RAINBOW

*"... Because the serpent made love to the rainbow
And the wind and water still wonder where their children have gone,
I've traveled across these roads of ancestral memory
to come and reclaim what my ancestors left for me. ... "*

He soothes me.
His lips bring peace,
calming the thunder that drowns my heartbeat.
Crocheting clouds into comfort,
his hands harness lightning.
Fingertips braiding fistfuls of air
into *rainbows*.
My baby's clothed in the colors that keep me faithful.
All I ever want to wear is him.
Says I am every woman he's ever dreamt about.
Chronicled each sighting in his diary,
then burned the book in offering to me.
He knew I would come.
Spinning the ashes into world winds,
he gives honor to his blessings
'cause he knows, in the beginning
it was God who first said to Her husband
"Let us make man in our image"

so from in between black thighs he did emerge
and into black thighs he will return
Anything less would be blasphemous.

And while his lineage ends on these North American shores
He understands every syllable of my Creole.
Tells me that my fried plantains,
diri au sous pois, codfish and malanga
remind him of a home long forgotten

and the rise and fall of my hips are reminiscent of the *rada* drum.

My after glow is the hum that lulls him to sleep.
Often times, before the cock crows,
he awakens to the sound of the Tom-tom beating
in my chest, and as his finger tips walk familiar
paths across the fullness of me I smile,
remembering lifetimes ago when we first met
and since how I've longer for those hands to reclaim my flesh.
I am his Iemanja, once removed,
reincarnated as the Virgin Mary,
only to be unveiled as Erzulie.
Agwe baptized me on the Atlantic coast of *Boyo Quis Queya, Ayiti.*

But it was on the upper east side of Manhattan that my *baby* found me.

His kisses reawaken dreams of *La citadel* and *San souci,*
midnight jasmine, and sour sop trees.
And I can hear the women marching
through my veins calling to me saying-

" *Cheri, he has come.*
He knows you by all your names
and wears them engraved underneath his tongue
so when you taste yourself familiar you'll remember,

he's journeyed the distance of history,
carrying the seeds of your love in his belly.

Petite mwen, when you look into his eyes
you'll see where your past lives are buried.
He has known you from the beginning
followed you from Eden and shared your throne in Dahomey.
Survived his passage through the middle of hell

*by wrapping himself in your memory.
And, Cheri, si ou pa sonje, on the night of the last rebellion,
 he held your heart in his hands
while you rode his hips into the dawn of revolution.
 Spinning visions of you into armor,
 it was your love that camouflaged him
the night he set the Cane fields on fire.*

*And we...we have transcended lifetimes to keep you together
Crossed and uncrossed unseen paths to make sure you'd find one another.
My daughter, peace and be still so you can remember
how your waters ached for lightening on the nights he spoke thunder.
And how on that day he laid himself
 on the bottom of Trujillo's Massacre River,
clutching your lifeless body as his anchor.
And we...we were slow to anger and never to blame him
Cause we knew he believed that was the only way
 to keep you from leaving again,
not knowing that your soul is eternally tied to his
and every reincarnation brings you back to him.*

*Cherie, it is only through the memory of your love
that we have come to live again."*

He says I am shaped like I should be sacred,
and when we make love he can feel generations move in between us.
Keeps his head on my chest,
says so he can hear the foot steps of our unborn children.

Palms pressed against my the arch of my back as our bodies replay the rhythm.
And as I drift off to sleep, I can hear the voices in our veins whisper in unison
"...Because the serpent made love to the rainbow

and the wind and water still wonder where their children have gone-
I've traveled across these roads of ancestral memory to come and reclaim what my ancestors left for me."

Christine-Jean Blain

WHAT MATTERS MOST

What would they say to us?
What would they say matters most when all is done
And said?
Bow your head
And thank the Most High for the pain that you feel
For if you can still feel it,
Then it means you surely must still be alive
...and what a miracle.
For the dead cannot feel sorrow.

Take these lessons and wear them like ornaments around
your neck,
Nose, ears, and wrists
Let them dangle when you walk
Let the glint of light reflect on these jewels
boldly as you talk
And speak your whole heart
while there are still words left to be
Spoken.
Run as fast as you can to your dreams
while there are still dreams to be caught
Run as fast as you can to the children,
while there are still children to be taught
LOVE as hard as you can,
and take the subsequent pain as evidence
That you're still living, that you are still giving fuel
to the fire of precedents,
These
Precedents of purpose
These precedents of strife
Be a daughter to your mother
Be a husband to your wife
Be everything you would want to be if you had a chance
to live again after dying.
If we could cross the barrier
between the living and the angels,

What would they say to us?
And
What would they say matters
Most
When it's all
Done
And
Said?

Stacey Lois Howard

SYMPATHY (*Circa 1899*)

I know what the caged bird feels, alas!
    When the sun is bright on the upland slopes;
    When the wind stirs soft through the springing grass,
And the river flows like a stream of glass;
    When the first bird sings and the first bud opes,
And the faint perfume from its chalice steals–
I know what the caged bird feels!

I know why the caged bird beats its wing
    Till its blood is red on the cruel bars;
    For he must fly back to his perch and cling
When he fain would be on the bough a-swing;
    And a pain still throbs in the old, old scars
And they pulse again with a keener sting–
I know why he beats his wing!

I know why the caged bird sings, ah me,
    When his wing is bruised and his bosom sore,–
    When he beats his bars and he would be free;
It is not a carol of joy or glee,
    But a prayer that he sends from his heart's deep core,
But a plea, that upward to Heaven he flings–
I know why the caged bird sings.

                              Paul Laurence Dunbar (1872-1906)

NOTES

Paul Laurence Dunbar (**1872-1906**) was born in Dayton, Ohio to former slaves. Dunbar published several collections of verse, including *Lyrics of Lowly Life* [1896], *Lyrics of the Hearthside* [1899], *Lyrics of Sunshine and Shadow* [1901], and *Lyrics of Love and Laughter* [1903]. He married poet Alice Ruth Moore in 1898, separating in 1902. Dunbar was a poet, novelist and short story writer and widely acknowledged as the first important black poet in American literature. He died in 1906 from tuberculosis at age 33.

CONTRIBUTORS

Cover
Kemi Aderibigbe is the artist responsible for the book's cover image, 'Reflections of Hope'. Kemi is an innovative artist who takes inspiration from people, her surroundings and life experience. Her passion for Art and Design stems from childhood, she has a degree in Fashion Design. Kemi favours ink, graphite, pencil, acrylic and oil paint as her preferred media and her work is characterized by bold use of shape, line and colour, which together, effectively capture expression and emotion.

Book Jacket Design
Danielle Humphrey has been a regular on the independent arts scene since 2003. She has worked as an Artistic Director for the BFM's (Black Filmmaker) International Film Festival publicity materials and was responsible for the design of several issues of the BFM magazine. In addition to her commercial work for B2B publications, Danielle has produced printed works for Images of Black Women Film Festival, Hatch Events and Screen Nation Film & TV Awards. Danielle has a BA (Hons) degree in Graphic design from Luton University and currently works as a freelance graphic designer for a consumer and trade publisher.

Writers

Christine-Jean Blain currently resides in Brooklyn, New York. She is of Afro-Carribean descent. She is an educator, writer and performer. With a graduate degree in Public Administration and Non-Profit Management, Christine-Jean worked in State and local government for a number of years, before moving into Education.

Christine is the author of *Lighting the Path Back Home,* a short collection of poetry and prose. Her work has been published in many magazines and newspapers such as African Voices and the ASP. She is a former Writer in Residence at Hedgebrook, a Cave Canem Alumna, and a founding member of Dusks Daughters Arts Collective.

Stacey Lois Howard is a poet, musician, and activist from Atlanta, Georgia, USA. She has performed in stage-plays such as "Take Our Youth Back", and "Get Out the Box", Stacey Louise Howard's poetry compilation *Spark in the Temple* will be released on the Urban Thought Books imprint.

Rene Thomas was born in Wigan. Rene currently lives in Huddersfield, and contributes to his community through political involvement and voluntary work, as well as through his art and writing.

Kamaria Muntu is an African American artist, poet and activist. She has completed a volume of **poetry**, and has two poems featured in *Call & Response: The Riverside Anthology of the African American Literary Tradition*, a critically acclaimed anthology used at Universities throughout the United States. Muntu has presented her work to audiences throughout the USA and Canada, most notably at the "National Black Arts Festival" in Atlanta Georgia, alongside the founders of "Black Arts Movement": Sonia Sanchez, Askia Toure, Amiri Baraka, Angela Jackson and Mari Evans. As part of her work as an activist, she has co-written a critique on The Million Man March, which is featured in the anthology, *Fertile Ground; Memories & Visions*. Mutu is a single mother to two grown children and now resides in London, where she has founded her own production company, Right Limb Films. She is currently editing a film she wrote and produced, entitled Les Morts: The Black Women.

Mbizo Chirasha is a writer and performance poet. He lives and works in Namibia and has worked with several organizations in and around Africa. "Haiti My Generation" was written on 27 January 2010 and was performed by Mbizo in Namibia at the Haiti Fundraising Gala dinner.

Lloyd Akinsanya Palmer hails from the garden parish of St. Ann and was born into hardworking rural family. Palmer views poetry as a holistic therapy which can spiritually uplift humanity. In 2005 he was second runner Up in the 7th Annual Writers' Award and in 2007 he was first Runner Up in the 9th Annual Writers' Award. Palmer released his debut album TUFF TUFF TRANGLE "Urban Journey" as a poet in 2005. He is currently working on his debut anthology *Sankofa* and also preparing for the release of his band's debut album "The Uprising Roots Band" debut album "Skyfiya".

Simon Murray -SaiMuRai is a writer, poet and artist of Bajan heritage. In 2009 he was commissioned for 'C Words' (an Artist-Activist project, Bristol), and was part of the 'F Words: Creative Freedom' USA tour 2008. As a poet-coach with Leeds Young Authors, his team has won the UK's leading Slam Festival, Voices of A New Generation, for the last 2 years. The first part of his debut novel, *Kill Myself Now: The True Confessions of an Advertising Genius* is published by Peepal Tree Press. http://www.myspace.com/saimuraiswords

Deka Ibrahim (See full bio under WAPPY Collective below)

Bob McNeil, Bob McNeil was born in New York City to a Saint Vincentian mother and an African-American father. Bob was the Poetry Editor for BLACFAX and has published two books: *Secular Sacraments,* and *The Nubian Gallery, A Poetry Anthology.* Both can be found in libraries, universities and bookstores. To date, he has been the Featured Poet at numerous libraries throughout the tri-state area. He also performs with his spoken word and music group, The Grande Beats.

Sophia Wilson is a prolific writer and performer. She facilitates creativity workshops and story telling to the young and not so young. She is the chairperson of Inspired Word, a women's writing collective in Lewisham, South East London.

Tolu Ogunlesi was born in 1982. He is a poet, photographer and journalist. His most recent book is *Conquest and Conviviality*, a novella for young adults (Hodder, 2008). He lives in Lagos, Nigeria. www.toluogunlesi.wordpress.com

Suzanne Creavalle writes poetry, fiction and autobiographical pieces. 'Morning Coffee' acknowledges the faith and strength of the Haitian people in the face of adversity. Her first published autobiographical work 'Afro Child' appears in the book, *Hair Power Skin Revolution*. Her interests include world dance and theatre, in particular Brazilian and African genres. Suzanne is of Guyanese descent and lives in Surrey.

Jeffrey Jaiyeola, also known as Plumbline, is a poet, songwriter, and spoken word artist. Jeffrey was born in Lagos, Nigeria. As a kid, he was influenced by local poets like the late Mamman Vatsa and the late Ken Saro Wiwa. He started writing from high school onwards. He performs Spoken Word Poetry at most Lagos Events like Wordslam, Anthill, Taruwa and hosts Chill and Relax, a poetry, comedy and light music event in Lagos, Nigeria.

Andy Nguyen 7th GRADER (**see bio under** Martin Luther King Jr Early College **below**)

Yolande M Deane is from Tottenham in North London and teaches English as a Foreign Language (EFL) in a language school in Central London. She has also taught English in Italy, where she lived for two years. She has been writing since she was a child.

Ann-Margaret Lim lives in Red Hills Jamaica. She has been published in the Caribbean Writer (2008, 2009, 2010), BIM, the Journal of Caribbean Literatures, Calabash: a Journal of Caribbean Arts and Letters, the Caribbean Quarterly, the Calabash poetry workshop anthology: *So Much Things To Say*; the Pittsburg Quarterly online, the Jamaica Gleaner and the Jamaica Observer, with upcoming work in WiSPA's MOTHERLOGUE Anthology and the Black Londoners' Haiti Anthology. She was the 2005 Red Bones Poet of the Year.

Opal Minott was born in Jamaica, where she has lived all her life. She is a medical social worker, wife, and mother of three. She has had a burning desire to write poetry from childhood and has been doing so since then.

Stephanie L Kemp is a writer originally from Seattle, WA. She has had her poems published in numerous journals and anthologies. She published her first book of poetry entitled *All's Fair* in 2009. She currently she lives in Colorado.

Uche Francis Uwadinachi is from Nigeria. She is a performance poet and the winner of ANA (Association of Nigerian Authors) Lagos poetry festival prize 2006 and Pakistan June-poetrycraze online contest 2009. She is the author of *Scar in the Heart of Pain*, collections of poetry (2009). She was the former Editor of AJ city Express Newspaper. Uche is also an actor and has appeared in Nigerian movies such as Real Love, Love of my Life, Adam and Eve and many others. Uche is currently

involved in a TV documentary, KONTO MUSIC
WEBSITE:http://www.flames777.blogspot.com
Email: flame45ng@yahoo.com

Lucreta La Pierre loves writing poetry and is especially fond of writing Creole based poetry. She started writing poetry in 2007, following a workshop on the slave trade, when she wrote her first poem "Ancestors". She was awarded an MBE in 2004 for voluntary services in Lewisham and further afield. La Pierre has also had some work published recently.

Nadine Pinede is the daughter of Haitian immigrants. She is a graduate of Harvard University and Oxford University, where she received her MA in English and Modern Languages as a Rhodes Scholar. She earned her PhD at Indiana University and is an Elizabeth George Foundation Scholar in the MFA program in Fiction at the Whidbey Writers Workshop. Her writing has appeared in numerous publications, including The New York Times, San Francisco Chronicle, Radcliffe Quarterly, Literary Newsmakers, Sampsonia Way, The Other Journal, and Soundings Review. Her poetry has been broadcast on Indiana Public Radio, and her play was featured in the Harvard Festival of One Acts. Nadine is a two-time grant recipient from the Indiana Arts Commission and has been a resident at Hedgebrook and an associate artist at the Atlantic Center for the Arts. Her short story, *Departure Lounge*, is forthcoming in Haiti Noir, edited by Edwidge Danticat.

Tade Thompson has been published in small press and online magazines, he is an artist and has illustrated eBook covers. He is a contributing author to the group blog 'In My Dreams it was Much Simpler' (also collected in book form) and administrator for the Nigerian Writers group. He has recently written and illustrated a children's book and is currently working on a novel. *Celeste*, his short story contribution to this anthology was inspired by the everyday struggles of the poor and disenfranchised in Haiti upon which the earthquake imposed catastrophic complications

Marcia Kay Ellis (See bio under WAPPY below)

Kathuska Jose was born in Port-au-Prince, Haiti on October 1986. She graduated from the University of Massachusetts, Amherst in May 2010 with a BA in English and a Specialization in Creative Writing. Her poems have appeared in *Jabberwocky, Short Cuts, Mother Tongue* and *Bang and Whimper*. She currently lives in Everett, Massachusetts.

Erline Vendredi
Erline is Haitian and was in Haiti during the earthquake of January 12 2010. She remained in Haiti for about three weeks until she returned to the US to resume her studies. Erline's contribution is a poem written in Creole with a loose English Translation to give non-Creole readers an idea of the Creole version.

Fitzroy Cole, also known as Jagga/Viva!, is the author of three anthologies - *Beloved Enemy* (1995), *Lyrical Sonnets from the Heart/Sojourner*(2005) and the third, *For the Sake Of Magic...Poetry Is Life*!(2009). *Lyrical Sonnets* is available at bazba.com and *For the Sake of Magic* is available from xlibris.com, barnesandnoble.com; amazon.com and borders.com. Fitzroy is also a performance poet and recently emigrated to Miami, Florida.
Geoffrey Philp is the author of a children's book, *Grandpa Sydney's Anancy Stories*, and a collection of short stories, *Who's Your Daddy?* His next collection of poems, *Dub Wise*, will be published by Peepal Tree Press in September 2010. He maintains a blog @ geoffreyphilp.blogspot.com

Tony Walsh is based in Manchester (UK) and has performed his poetry both nationally and internationally, from the Glastonbury Festival in the United Kingdom, to the Palace of Culture and Science in Warsaw, Poland. Widely published in the UK, Tony's poetry has recently been published for the first time in the USA.

Alexander Thanni, a.k.a. The Reverend, is an orator, narrator and social commentator on subjects ranging from social alienation to self determination. He is an up and coming spoken word artist and has performed at a range of events, from art gallery openings to the well known Word Play. Alexander is 24 years of age and lives in North London. He is part of the Plantain Collective.

Akilah Moseley is a trainer, executive coach, leadership mentor and emerging writer and poet. Since 2007 she has been an active member of the Ispired Word poetry collective. Akilah has performed her poetry widely across London. Her first anthology *Thoughts from a reasoning Mind*, was compiled in 2008. Her work has also appeared in the 2009 Inspired Word anthology *Sharing Space*. Most recently Akilah collaborated with 7 other authors in writing *I Factor for women* (2010). Akilah can be contacted at akilahmoseley@yahoo.co.uk or Akilah@lineone.net

Acquaye McCalman (see bio under WAPPY)

Nadifa Mohamed was born in Hargesia, Somalia in 1981 and was educated in the UK, studying History and Politics at St Hilda's College, Oxford. Her debut novel, *Black Mamba Boy* recounts the epic journey of the author's father through war-torn Eritrea and Sudan, to Egypt, Palestine and finally to Britain. *Black Mamba* Boy was longlisted for the Orange Prize and Dylan Thomas Prize and won the 2010 Betty Trask Prize. She lives in London and is currently working on her second novel.

Maroula Blades is an Afro-British poet/writer living in Berlin. Verbrecher Verlag, TAZ and Cornelsen Verlag have published her stories. Her poems have been published in Germany and abroad and she has received awards for her work. Blades was awarded the runner's up prize for the GC Chapbook UK 2008 and was the featured poet in the Erbacce 16 2009. Her Poetry/Music Programme has already been presented on several stages in Berlin: the Planetarium am Insulaner, IFA, Der Haus der Kulturen der Welt and Volksbühne among others. Maroula has read at the Black History Month Festival 2010 in Berlin and at the Berlin Poetry Festival 2010.

Nick Falconer (see bio under Martin Luther King Jr Early College **below**)

Esther Ackah (see bio under WAPPY below)

Kwame M.A. McPherson is an author, poet, motivational speaker, entrepreneur and mentor. He began writing as a hobby from a young age whilst living in Jamaica. He is the author of two volumes of work; *Our Eternal Legacy*, a compilation published in November 2007 and *Deep Roots, Strong Tree*, a collection of short stories which was published in April 2008. His latest works, *Yawd Vibes* and *To Our Fallen* will be published in 2010/11. Kwame has written for Candace Magazine (London), AFAR (Connecticut, USA) and has featured on television and radio.

Nicole Weaver (see bio under Martin Luther King Jr. Early College **below**)

Lane Ashfeldt's short fiction has been published online and in anthologies from *Punk Fiction* to *Dancing With Mr. Darcy*. Awards for her short fiction include the Fish Short Histories Prize, a Hawthornden Fellowship and a Jane Austen Short Story Award. Lane grew up in London and Dublin and has lived and worked in several European countries. www.ashfeldt.com

RaShell R. Smith-Spears grew up in Memphis, Tennessee. She received her B.A. from Spelman College and her graduate degrees from The University of Memphis and University of Missouri-Columbia. She currently teaches American, African-American, and World Literature classes at Jackson State University in Jackson, Mississippi. She has been published in *Black Magnolias Literary Journal*, *Short Story* and *Writing African-American Women*.

Phil Gregory
Phil Gregory is the owner/Editor of Blackpresence.co.uk a website highlighting black History worldwide. When not writing for Blackpresence he is an Educator, active blogger and writer for Political website Pitsnpots. Phil enjoys photography and works freelance as an Apple Distinguished Educator training students in Digital media across the world.

Olufemi Amao is a lecturer at Brunel Law School, West London.

Georgina Jackson-Callen (see bio under WAPPY below)

Nash Colundalur is a writer, journalist and architect. He writes poetry and short fiction as well as writing on social and development issues for the Guardian and other international publications. In 2009 he won the Guardian International Development Journalism Award for reporting on the drought in northern Kenya.

Margaret Danquah is currently working as a careers adviser in Higher Education. She has taken part in The Poetry Society's competition and last year's Aesthetica Magazine Creative Works competition, among others. She enjoys poetry, theatre and art and her literary influences include Linton Kwesi Johnson and Benjamin Zephaniah.

Jai Ellis-Crook (see bio under WAPPY below)

David Larbi (see bio under WAPPY below)

Abigail Perry Duah (see bio under WAPPY below)

LaTrell Johnson (see bio under Martin Luther King Jr. Early College below)

Kathy Cakebread has been writing for approximately ten years and has written a number of works including both short stories and novellas.

The Writing, Acting and Publishing Project for Youngsters (WAPPY)

Akuba (Grace Quansah)
Akuba was born in London and is an award-winning literary artiste of Ghanaian descent. In 2008, she founded the Writing, Acting and Publishing Project for Youngsters (WAPPY), which is supported by the Positive Awareness Charity and Ealing Council. As well as managing the project, Akuba works as a facilitator with the British Museum. She has had seventeen pieces of literature published in various anthologies and journals including Journey's Home (U.S.A. 2009).

Abigail Perry (11 years old)
Abigail Perry was born in London to Ghanaian parents and spent her early childhood in Ghana. She is 11 years old and is a Year 6 student of Berrymede Primary School in Ealing. She loves sports, reading and creative writing and would like to read medicine when she is older. She has been a member of WAPPY since 2009.

Acquaye McCalman (16 years old)
Acquaye McCalman was born in London and is of Ghanaian and Guyanese descent. He is 16 years old and has just completed his GCSEs at Drayton Manor High School in Ealing. He will begin a B'Tech Diploma in Music in September 2010

David Larbi (12 years old)
David Larbi was born in London and is a Year 7 pupil of John Lyons School, Hillingdon, where he recently received three awards for his outstanding abilities in Drama, English and PE. He is 12 years old and wrote his poem after watching a Channel Four Dispatches program on the situation in Zimbabwe.

Deka Ibrahim
Born in Saudi Arabia, Deka Ibrahim came to the UK at a young age, speaking mainly Arabic. She subsequently read English Literature and Language at King's College, University of London. Deka is a volunteer for WAPPY and her main inspiration is her late father, also a writer in his mother tongue. She hopes to pursue a career in journalism and creative writing.

Esther Ackah
Esther Ackah was born and raised in Ghana. She came to London in 1957. She has forty five years experience working for the National Health Service as a midwife, retiring in 2008. In her sixties, she gained a degree in Theology and Sociology at Roehampton Institute in 1998, and a diploma in Counselling in 2002. Also an accredited Methodist Lay Preacher since 2002, Esther's faith in God motivated her to write 'A Prayer for Haiti' to uplift the spirit of the Haitian people in this difficult time. Esther is a grandmother and is 75 years of age.

Georgiana Jackson-Callen (15 years old)
"Known as 'Georgie' by her friends, Georgiana Jackson-Callen is a Londoner of Jamaican and Ugandan heritage. She is fifteen years old. Her favourite subject is Spanish, she enjoys reading manga and Marvel comics, drawing, training for judo, singing and playing air guitar to a Hendrix standard. She was published in Time Out in 2009.

Jai Ellis-Crook (10 years old)
Jai Ellis – Crook was born in London, of Caribbean and English parentage. She is ten years old and is a Year 5 student at Mayfield Primary School in Ealing. Jai loves writing stories.

Marcia K Ellis
Marcia Kay Ellis was born in London in 1965, of Jamaican parentage. She is a painter and creative artist by profession. Marcia was inspired to write her debut poem, Wake Up Haiti! through her involvement as a WAPPY parent member. View her work at:www.marciarts.co.uk

Martin Luther King Jr Early College, Denver, Colorado
Contributions from Teacher and Students:

Nicole Weaver (Teacher) teaches at Martin Luther King Jr Early College in Denver Colorado. She was born in Port-au-Prince Haiti. She came to the United States when she was ten years old. She is fluent in Creole, French, Spanish and English. She teaches French and Spanish. She is the author of a children's trilingual picture book titled *Marie and Her Friend the Sea Turtle*. Her second trilingual children's picture book *My sister is my Best Friend* will be published fall 2010.

Latrell Johnson: 10th Grader

Tanya Leon, 9th Grader

Andy Nguyen 7th Grader

Nick Falconer, 7th Grader